HUNTER

IRON ROGUES MC

FIONA DAVENPORT

Copyright © 2025 by Fiona Davenport

Cover designed by Elle Christensen

Edited by Jenny Sims (Editing4Indies)

All rights reserved.

No part of this book may be reproduced in any form or by any electronic or mechanical means, including information storage and retrieval systems, without written permission from the author, except for the use of brief quotations in a book review.

❀ Created with Vellum

HUNTER
IRON ROGUES MC

As an enforcer for the Iron Rogues MC, Wesley "Hunter" Hastings was used to maintaining order. But his self-control flew out the window when he laid eyes on Sadie Carter. The pretty baker was young, sweet, and too damn innocent. But that wasn't going to stop him from claiming her.

Sadie didn't have any experience with men like Hunter. But when trouble found her, the grumpy biker showed her exactly how far he'd go to make sure nothing touched what was his.

1

SADIE

Today was my first real day of work, and I was a weird mixture of excited and nervous. The steering wheel was damp under my palms, my nerves making my hands a little sweaty as I made the twenty-five-minute drive to Country Crust.

It was a gorgeous day with only a few fluffy clouds in the early morning sky, but the nice weather did nothing to soothe the anxious flutter under my ribs. Everything had happened so quickly that I hadn't really had time to get nervous until now.

This wasn't a babysitting gig for one of my neighbors or helping out as a volunteer at the library for a few hours each week. I had actually landed a full-time job doing something I loved, but it came with responsibilities, a boss, and customers.

My phone rang through the car speakers, and I grinned when I saw on the dashboard that my mom was calling. Tapping the button on my steering wheel, I answered, "Hey, Mom!"

"Hi, honey! We woke up early so we could call before you started your big day," she chirped.

Since they were two hours behind me and I had just talked to them last night, their thoughtfulness meant even more to me. "That's so sweet, thank you."

"We couldn't let our baby's big day pass by without any fanfare."

She sniffled, so I changed the topic of conversation to avoid her getting all teary over me having my first real job.

"How's the newest campground?" I asked, turning onto the street that led into the heart of Old Bridge, a few towns over from where I lived with my parents in the same house I'd grown up in.

"Your dad tried to hook up the sewer line to the wrong tank," she informed me with a giggle.

I laughed. "Oh no."

"Oh yes. Let's just say he had to take a very long shower afterward," she added, still laughing. "Poor guy has experienced all the steepest learning curves since we hit the road. The whole thing seemed so much easier from our driveway."

"I'm sure it did." Even if the thought of being crammed into an RV for weeks made my skin crawl, hearing about their silly misadventures almost made me wish that I had gone with them. "I miss you guys."

"We miss you too, honey. So much." My mom's voice turned wistful as she murmured, "You would've loved Yosemite, you know. The waterfalls were incredible. Your father kept grumbling about the crowds, but I caught him smiling like a kid half the time."

"Hey!" Dad called out in the background. "I can appreciate nature."

"Just not the parking lot," Mom teased as she switched the call to speakerphone.

"Too many damn cars when you're driving a rig as big as ours," he muttered.

"But that's not the part of our trip that you'll be the most interested in," my mom blurted. "For dinner last night, we stopped at this little place you'd go nuts for. It's the oldest restaurant in Arizona, Rock Springs Café. They've been open since 1918. Can you believe it?"

"Wow," I breathed as I turned onto Main Street. "That's a long time."

"We tasted for ourselves how they've managed to stay in business for so long. They're famous for their pies," my dad announced. "Best bourbon pecan pie I've ever had. The guy said the secret is the water because the town is right over an aquifer."

"Please," Mom huffed. "The mixed berry pie was better."

"Sadie would have loved the pecan," Dad insisted.

My mom didn't cave. "The berry was named Arizona's centennial pie for a reason."

Knowing they would bicker back and forth like this for an hour if I let them, I gasped dramatically. "But is it better than my chess pie?"

"Hmm," my dad hummed, drawing out his answer to tease me.

"Absolutely not," Mom said loyally. "Your chess pie wins every time, honey."

I'd made that recipe with her every holiday and birthday since I was tall enough to see the counter. I laughed, warmth blooming in my chest. "I guess I'll just have to settle the debate myself someday."

"We should've overnighted you a slice," Dad grumbled good-naturedly.

"Circle around there again when you're on your way back," I suggested.

"Great idea," my mom agreed. "But for now, don't worry about how delicious that slice of mixed berry pie will be. Instead, focus on making it through your big day. I can't believe you barely had the chance to start your job search and already found one where you start so quickly."

Even though they couldn't see me, I shrugged. "Like I explained yesterday, I couldn't resist stopping into the bakery when I saw their post about the soft opening and somehow walked away with a job to go along with my delicious butter pecan cookie."

"Because you're a sweetheart who loves baking," Mom said.

"We're proud of you, honey," my dad added. "And happy you found something close to home."

I wasn't surprised that was the most important part for him. My parents had me later in life, and I was an only child, so they were more than a little overprotective. "Me too."

"Now go knock 'em dead, sweetheart."

My parents' pep talk gave me the courage to climb out of my car and head into the bakery, an hour ahead of its seven o'clock opening. The warm smell of vanilla and sugar wrapped around me instantly. Yeasty bread, sweet icing, and a hint of cinnamon hung in the air, making my stomach rumble. A soft clatter came from the walk-in fridge.

"Good morning, Marcy," I called.

My new boss stepped into my line of vision, carrying a stack of egg cartons. "Morning, Sadie! Ready to get to work?"

"I sure am." I beamed a big smile at her. "Where do you want me?"

"After you put your stuff in the office for safe-keeping, please get to work on loading the muffins into the display case. Oh and if you see a young guy lingering about, just ignore him. Austin is fixing the leaky air-conditioning." She laughed and shrugged. "I guess it was too much to ask that the opening go perfectly. But he'll have it done in a jiffy, so just work around him."

"Will do."

After I had added the trays of cookies, brownies, and cupcakes to the shelves next to the muffins, I joined her in the kitchen. "Need any help in here?"

She paused the commercial mixer and asked, "How are you at frosting cakes?"

"Pretty darn good, if I do say so myself."

I wasn't normally one to brag, but frosting was one of my favorite things, so I had spent many hours perfecting my skills. Something I proved over the next fifteen minutes. But I didn't have time to properly appreciate the pretty pink cake that I decorated because I finished only a few minutes before the doors opened.

Just then, a young blond guy popped into the kitchen. "All done, Marcy. Let me know if you need anything else."

"Thanks, Austin. Tell your dad to send me the bill."

His curious gaze landed on me, and Marcy quickly introduced us. He was the son of the local hardware store owner and the town's resident Mr. Fix-it.

He smiled warmly at me and shook my hand. I shifted edgily when he lingered just a little longer than usual.

"Well, we need to get ready to open," Marcy informed him before ushering him to the back door. She and I headed to the front of the bakery as she explained, "We're keeping things simple this first week. I'll work the register and espresso machine. You stock, serve, and help out wherever. Once the dust settles, I'll have you help with the baking, too."

I nodded and tried to sound more confident than I felt when I replied, "Got it."

"Don't worry, you'll pick it up fast," she assured me with a smile.

Appreciating her confidence in me, I grinned back at her. "Good. Because if you need someone to bake a hundred cupcakes in an afternoon, I'm your girl. But if you want fancy barista moves, I will definitely need some lessons."

Marcy laughed. "We'll get there."

She ran me through the basics quickly—how to use the POS system, where the extra cups and napkins were, and how she wanted the pastries boxed up. It was a lot, but it felt good. Like being here was the perfect fit for me. Except then she said something that made me worry a little.

"And be extra nice to any customer you see wearing an Iron Rogues MC vest."

My brows drew together. "I don't even know what that is."

Her eyes widened. "They're the motorcycle club that basically owns all of Old Bridge, including this building. I figured with you growing up a few towns over, you'd at least have heard of them before."

I shook my head, picturing a gang of rough-looking bikers like something out of the movies. "Are they dangerous?"

Marcy shrugged. "Depends on who you ask. If

you're causing trouble around here? Very. For a cute girl like you who's just baking cookies and minding your business? Nah."

"Oh good."

Marcy bumped my shoulder lightly. "Unless one of them falls for you. Then they're the very best kind of trouble."

I scoffed at the thought of attracting the attention of a man like she had just described. "I don't see that happening."

"You'd be very lucky if it did. Behind the leather and tattoos, those men turn into big teddy bears when they claim their old lady." She fanned herself with her hand. "And if any of them brings one of the babies in, your ovaries are sure to explode."

2

HUNTER

"Hunter."

Halfway past Fox's office, I heard him call my name. He was the president of my club, the Iron Rogues, so I pivoted and stepped inside. Stone, our captain and club lawyer, was kicked back in a chair beside Fox's desk, flipping through a packet of papers.

Fox sat behind a desk you'd expect to see in a Wall Street exec's office—big, modern, and spotless. He was a neat freak to the core, though only Maverick, our VP and his best friend, had the balls to tease him about it. The rest of us valued breathing too much.

The prez was wicked smart, had a head for numbers, and a gift for strategy. A complete nerd.

But he'd also been schooled in martial arts and weapons from a young age and was deadlier and more fucking ruthless than most of the guys in the club.

Yeah, his road name was spot on. Intelligent, cunning, and lethal.

Before patching into the club, he'd earned a degree in finance from an Ivy League university. Then he'd spent a few years cleaning up on Wall Street. After making a few million, he got bored and came home. Despite being the son of one of the founders—and the president at the time—Fox had prospected like the rest of us, earning fear and respect as he worked his way to the top.

Now? He was the reason we owned most of Old Bridge—and a nice chunk of the next few towns over.

Fox was talking with Maverick, who was leaning against the desk, arms crossed. Deviant, and Racer—two of our enforcers—were camped out at the round table in the corner. So was Savage, a patch who managed the club's bar, The Midnight Rebel.

The room was built to accommodate large gatherings. Oversized, with a bar and a couple of battered sofas, plus a side door leading into Mav's office.

"Need something?" I grunted.

Fox paused, pinning me with his steady, sharp gaze. "Need you to make a stop on your way out."

I nodded.

Viper and I had a quick run to make—delivering a sensitive package to a customer—and then I planned to take a few extra days for a ride-out. It had been almost a year since I'd taken time off. Being an enforcer, especially one with my...skill set, kept me tied up more often than not. Fox gave me shit about burnout every so often, but he wasn't the type to hold my hand. Which I appreciated because after fifteen years split between the military and the FBI, I didn't need anyone telling me when to eat, sleep, or shit.

When I'd mentioned taking a break, he just grunted, "'Bout fucking time."

Stone unfolded from his chair and held out the packet of papers, so I crossed the room and took them.

One glance had my brows pulling together. "A rental agreement?"

Sniper rifles, tracking ghosts, interrogation—those were my wheelhouse. I was a fucking trained killer who was one of the best shots in the country. Legal paperwork? Not so much.

"Just have it with you," Stone said as though it made perfect sense. "In case there's any questions."

I scanned the document again. "Country Crust," I muttered, then shot Fox a look. "The new bakery?"

He nodded. "When the owner signed the lease, we slipped in a clause allowing background checks on new hires."

Savage whistled low. "She actually agreed to that?"

Stone shrugged. "Don't think she noticed. Her lawyer didn't object. Wasn't my job to point it out."

"She hired someone a couple of days ago," Fox added.

I waited, silent. Wasting words wasn't my style. It had served me well when I was growing up—and in my career—since being invisible had been an asset in both environments.

Fox was used to it, so he went on without being prompted.

"She hired the girl on the spot. No application, no system record. No name, no social. Until the paperwork's filled out and we can dig deeper, we need to get a read on her."

There it was. The reason I was being sent on this little errand.

Maverick spoke up. "Doubt you'll have to show it, but if the owner pitches a fit about you sniffing around, flash the lease."

Racer chuckled. "Or turn on that Hunter charm."

"Guys don't need charm when they look like him," Molly—Maverick's old lady—teased as she breezed into the room.

She winked at me, and Mav's growl sent a chill through my bones. My club brothers weren't reasonable when it came to their women. They'd lost their fucking minds.

"You trying to get my ass kicked?" I muttered.

"She's aiming for a cherry-red ass," Maverick snarled, hauling his wife into his arms.

"What makes you think I wasn't talking about you?" Molly shot back, laughing. Mav didn't crack a smile, but Molly smirked. "Will telling you that Luna is having a sleepover with your parents tonight get me out of trouble?"

"Nope," he grunted as he jumped to his feet and stalked out of the room with her slung over his shoulder.

"Lucky me!" Molly's giggles echoed down the hall.

Fox and Stone exchanged looks, both wearing the long-suffering smirks of men who knew exactly what it meant to be whipped—and didn't give a damn.

"Back to the job?" I prompted, not bothering to mask my impatience.

Deviant snorted. "Someone needs to get your grumpy ass a woman."

"Doesn't Alice know someone—" Racer started.

"Not a fucking chance in hell," I growled. I wasn't about to let Deviant's wife or anyone else set me up.

Deviant leaned back in his chair. "You don't trust Alice?"

I'd almost have believed he was truly offended on her behalf if his eyes hadn't been filled with laughter.

"It's not Alice I don't trust," I shot back. "It's you jackasses. Not gonna give you the chance to fuck with me."

Deviant shrugged. "Fair enough."

"Killjoy," Racer griped.

"Guess she'll just have to fix you up instead," Deviant drawled with a wicked grin.

Racer went on the defensive, but I ignored their banter and turned back to Fox.

"That all?"

He nodded. "Get a read on her. Call me before you and Viper roll out."

I gave him a chin lift and stalked out.

OUTSIDE THE GARAGE, Viper was already mounted and waiting.

"Fox mention our stop?" He sounded about as thrilled about the task as I was. This was understandable, considering that his old lady, Rhiannon, was about to pop with their first kid.

"Quick in and out," I promised.

He nodded grimly and kick-started his Harley, the vintage bike roaring to life while I threw a leg over mine. We pulled out and, a few minutes later, rolled up to Country Crust.

Our businesses weren't jammed onto the compound like some clubs. We owned a good chunk of Old Bridge, leasing out most of it, but the two-block radius around the clubhouse was all us.

Our own little kingdom had residential buildings and houses for members—and trusted tenants—plus the tattoo shop, bar, garage, pawn shop, gun range, barbershop...and more.

Country Crust was one of the few exceptions.

Big picture windows flanked a frosted door, each filled with displays that made my stomach growl.

Viper chuckled, and I shrugged. "Missed breakfast."

He nodded at one window and grinned. "If any of that shit tastes half as good as it looks, Rhiannon's cravings alone will keep 'em in business."

We stepped inside, and the smells of sugar, vanilla, and cinnamon hit me all at once. But something else was sweet and pure. I couldn't place it, but it only added to the alluring scents making my mouth water, and I damn near groaned out loud.

The place was busy but not packed, the kind of steady hum that meant the food was as delicious as it looked.

I lifted my chin at the people who called out greetings or nodded as I passed, heading straight for the front counter. Some of the customers scattered when they caught sight of my cut like they thought I was gonna snap and kill them for no fucking reason. Idiots.

Most folks in Old Bridge knew better. They understood the truth—there was no safer place to be than under the Iron Rogues' protection.

We lived by a code. Honor. Loyalty. Our own brand of justice.

We didn't take shit. And we sure as hell didn't leave it up to the authorities to deal with the ones stupid enough to cross us. Not that the cops minded much. The smart ones worked with us—because they knew better. The rest? We either owned them outright, or they looked the other way when we handled business.

Anyone dumb enough to fuck with us learned really quick that it was the last thing they'd ever do.

Crime didn't last long in Old Bridge.

Not unless we allowed it.

As I approached the counter, that smell that I couldn't place went straight to my bloodstream like a fucking drug.

Out of habit, I automatically scanned the room, and when the woman behind the counter caught my eye, the world went fucking still.

That scent...it was all her.

Soft curves tucked into a simple pale-yellow T-shirt and jeans. Light brown hair that was twisted into a messy bun. Blue eyes like the summer sky after a storm twinkled as she smiled at the customer in front of her. And those lips...holy fuck. They were made for kissing. And they were gonna look perfect wrapped around my cock.

The thought shocked the hell out of me and sent all the blood in my brain rushing to my dick.

Her eyes met mine for just a moment, then her face heated, the pale skin turning bright pink before she looked away. When she brushed a hand over her cheek, a dusting of flour was left behind, and one corner of my mouth lifted. Adorable.

Mine.

The thought hit so fast and vicious, it stole my breath. Tension pulled tight, hard, and fast in my chest—like someone had looped a fucking chain around my ribs.

Viper chuckled beside me. "You good, brother?"

I didn't answer. Couldn't get a fucking word out if I'd cared to try.

All I could do was stare, rooted to the spot like someone seeing sunshine for the first time in his shadowy life. I probably should have worried about what her light might reveal if it shined onto the deepest, darkest parts of me. But I was riveted, still lost to the vision before me.

She glanced at me again, and her body practically vibrated with bouncy, nervous energy. Almost as though she couldn't stand still but wasn't sure if she should run either.

And that blush...it was killing me. She was a shy, sweet thing—practically made of sunshine.

She was also young. Too damn young. *Fuck.*

I caught the slight twitch in her fingers when she brushed flour off her hands—and I nearly smiled at the tell. She was nervous, but when I looked closer, she didn't seem scared.

Big fucking difference.

Then her gaze darted behind me, and a shadow passed over her face. When I glanced back, the room was mostly clear, so all she was looking at was the door. Her eyes darted to the side door, as if she needed to know where the exits were. It was quick and subtle, but I hadn't missed a single thing about her since the moment I saw her and instinct crawled up my spine.

She was scared. Not of me, though. Not even today, not here—but at some point. Something had scarred her. And the fucking thought of it made my vision go a little red at the edges.

Some people might have missed the signs—but as I watched her and saw the way her breath sped up when too many people crowded the counter, how her gaze snagged on the closed kitchen door behind her, just for a second.

I rarely missed shit. I was quiet, observant, and had an unusual ability to read people. It was why Fox sent me to the bakery.

And it hadn't escaped my scrutiny that she hated feeling trapped.

Noted, sunshine.

Finally, the customer in front of me moved out of the way, and I stepped up to the counter. I was close enough to fill my lungs with her delicious aroma but not to touch her, and it drove me crazy.

"Hello, sunshine," I said, my voice low and rumbly. My lips curled up when I saw her tiny shiver and the pink blooming on her cheeks again.

She was affected by me. Good.

"Um. Hi. What can I get for you?"

Now, that was a loaded question if ever I heard one. What could she get for me?

Get on her knees.

Get naked.

Get bent over the nearest table.

Get fucked.

But rather than say what I was thinking and scare her off, I took a deep breath and focused on her soft voice and sweet smile.

"What's your name?" I asked as I swiped a couple of fingers over her cheek to brush away the residual flour. She shivered again, and I had to bite back a groan.

"Sadie Morgan."

"Beautiful," I murmured.

A muffled chuckle came from beside me, and I glanced over to see Viper watching me with amusement. I scowled, my eyes promising death and dismemberment if he said one fucking word.

He grinned and turned to Sadie. "Hi, Sadie. I'm Viper. How about a black coffee and one of those croissants? To go."

"Um, sure," she replied, stealing another glance at me before she turned to get Viper's order. There had been a glimmer of disappointment in her sky-blue orbs, and I was very tempted to reassure her that I wasn't going anywhere.

"You know we can't stay," Viper muttered, somehow reading my thoughts. As though I didn't fucking know that.

"Two days," I grunted.

A lot could happen in that time. What if some asshole decided he wanted her, and I wasn't around to officially stake my claim?

Viper nodded, knowing my mind again. "Send a text to one of the prospects and get them to cover the bakery until we get back. Tell 'em to scare the living shit out of any guy who goes near her."

Nodding, I withdrew my phone from the inner pocket of my cut and followed Viper's suggestion.

When I pressed send, some of the tension in my chest eased.

"Here you go," Sadie chirped as she handed my brother a to-go cup and paper bag. Then she turned her eyes back to my face and smiled. Any blood that had returned to my brain was now swelling my cock.

Fuck! What the hell had happened to my self-control? No one had ever been able to shake it before. Then along came this pretty, innocent little thing, and I was ready to snap.

"Do you want anything?" she pressed.

"You have to stop asking men shit like that," I grumbled. "It puts dirty ideas in their head."

Her mouth formed a little O, and she double blinked.

"Coffee, sunshine," I finally ordered, steering us away from the sexual tension building in the air.

"Black?" she asked breathlessly.

"Yeah, baby," I confirmed. "Black."

Just like my fucking soul.

Sadie beamed at me before grabbing a cup and the coffee pot.

"New around here?"

"Sort of," she answered with a smile as she poured, then replaced the pot and reached for a lid.

"I grew up twenty-five minutes from here, but I've never actually been to Old Bridge."

I cocked my head to the side. "Can't have been to many places at your age."

Sadie quirked a brow and giggled as she grabbed a frosted sugar cookies from the display case. "How did you know that?"

"I'm good at reading people," I admitted. "This is your first job."

She blushed and shuffled on her feet. "Am I that bad at it?"

"You're perfect, sunshine. An open book. I like seeing your thoughts and emotions so clearly on your face. But then again, at eighteen"—I guessed—"you haven't really learned to close yourself off yet."

"I'm nineteen," she corrected with a frown. "And that sounds lonely."

"Can be," I acknowledged. "Doubt anyone would feel that way around you, shining so bright."

"Um, thank you." She placed one of the sugar cookies—frosted in bright yellow—in a small bag and handed it to me.

I reached into my pocket for my wallet, but she waved it away.

"My treat." Her face flushed as she smiled bashfully. "A little sunshine to take with you."

"Thank you," I murmured. Our fingers brushed when she handed me the cup and cookie.

Electricity raced over every nerve ending, and it took every single shred of my control not to leap over that counter, throw her over my shoulder, and run.

"Hunter," Viper interrupted, his tone apologetic. "Gotta run, brother."

My hand flexed, itching to wrap around his neck and strangle him so he'd stop trying to drag me away from my sweet girl. Unfortunately, he wasn't wrong. And killing him in front of Sadie would probably make claiming her a fuck of a lot harder. I didn't want her to be afraid of me. Ever. I wanted to be the one to take away all of her fears.

First, I had to get this club shit out of the way. Since I'd already been planning to take a few days off when I got back, now I could devote all that time to her.

"Soon, sunshine," I told her in a low, gritty voice. My lips twitched when she shivered and blushed.

After looking her over once more, etching her face into my fucking bones, I turned and walked away.

Sadie Morgan was pure sunshine.

I felt a little unbalanced for the first time since I

was seventeen. But from the first moment I laid eyes on Sadie, I'd known one thing for certain.

She didn't belong to this place, this bakery, this town.

Sadie belonged to me.

She just didn't know it yet.

3
_____

SADIE

The alarm on my cell buzzed, and I blinked up at the ceiling, already wide awake even though it was only six o'clock in the morning.

I'd barely slept. Every time I closed my eyes, I pictured Hunter.

He hadn't said much when he was at the bakery yesterday, but that hadn't lessened his impact. I didn't think any woman would blame me for wondering about the tall, broad-shouldered biker.

He struck me as the strong, silent type. The kind of man who didn't need to say much because just being there was enough. At least for me.

It wasn't because I'd been scared, except maybe for my reaction to him because I had never felt a magnetic pull like this toward a guy before. I hadn't been able to get his tall, muscular body out of my head. Or his thick black hair, beard, and kissable lips.

And then there was his piercing amber gaze. I'd never seen eyes quite the same color before. They were wild and sharp, almost animalistic. Like a lion sizing up something he wanted. Not that I actually thought he wanted me when he could probably have any woman he set his sights on.

He was easily over a decade older than me and drop-dead gorgeous. Not the kind of man who noticed someone like me. But for a second, when our fingers had touched while I handed over his coffee and cookie, I could have sworn that I caught the barest flicker of something.

He'd only been at the bakery for maybe fifteen minutes, but that had been just long enough to set my entire world spinning. And it felt as though it hadn't stopped yet.

I was too inexperienced to know what my type was, but I never would have thought it to be a tatted-up biker. We were so different; even calling us opposites didn't seem like enough. But that didn't stop me from wondering about him. Which I didn't have time to do if I wanted to make it to my second day of work on time.

Groaning, I rolled out of bed and shuffled to the

bathroom, splashing cold water on my face in a futile attempt to knock some sense into myself.

"Get it together, Sadie," I muttered at my reflection.

I needed to focus. Just because I had another shift at the bakery today didn't mean that Hunter would show up again. Replaying his low, rumbling "thank you" over and over in my head wouldn't make him magically appear. No matter how much I wished otherwise.

After quickly getting ready, I snatched my keys off the counter and headed out the door. I spent the entire drive to the bakery reminding myself that I needed to focus on my job. Staring at the door all day would only get me fired.

Unfortunately, my heart didn't listen.

I parked behind the bakery and let myself in through the back door, breathing in the sweet, yeasty smell that had already begun to fill the air. Marcy was in the kitchen, pulling a tray of blueberry muffins out of the oven, her hair tucked under a pink bandanna.

"Morning, Sadie," she called without turning around.

"Good morning!" I replied, dropping my bag in

the office before washing my hands and grabbing an apron.

The front of the bakery was still quiet, and out of habit, my gaze darted to each door, reminding myself that I wasn't trapped before my anxiety got the best of me.

Then I set about loading fresh pastries into the display case. It was only my second day, but I already moved on autopilot, arranging trays of croissants and cinnamon rolls next to the items similar to what we'd carried yesterday.

When I was done, I went back to the kitchen, rubbing my palms together. "Good call on the new additions. Those cinnamon rolls look so ooey and gooey, it was hard not to sneak a taste."

"Then it's a good thing I already saved you one." Marcy jerked her head toward a small bakery box on the counter. "All ready for you to take home if you don't get the chance to nibble on it throughout the day."

I beamed a grateful smile at her. "Thank you."

"Consider free baked goods a perk of being my best employee."

"I'm your only employee," I pointed out with a giggle.

"For now." She pointed at a tray of chocolate

cupcakes. "Frost those the way you did that cake yesterday, and I bet they'll sell out before noon."

It didn't take me long to finish, and Marcy made a beeline over to my side to look the cupcakes over.

"Great job." Marcy patted me on the back. "Keep up the good work, and you won't be my only employee for long."

She was proven right about how quickly the cupcakes were gone. Five hours after we opened the doors, the case didn't have much left.

Even with how busy we were, every time the bell over the door jingled, my heart jumped. But I never spotted Hunter. I told myself that was a good thing because I needed to focus on my job. Not get distracted by a man who probably hadn't thought twice about the shy bakery girl who gave him a cookie.

I felt a little guilty about not being as attentive to the customers as I usually was. Especially when Austin stopped by. He'd come in every day for a coffee and always took a few minutes to talk with me. He was nice enough, but there was no spark. Not like the fire that consumed me when a certain sexy biker was around. Austin had tried to ask me out a few times, but I'd managed to sidestep it. We were becoming friends, though, so I felt bad when he left looking so disappointed today.

I must not have hidden my anxiousness to see Hunter very well because when we finally slowed down, Marcy leaned her elbows on the counter and grinned. "Expecting someone?"

My cheeks heated, and I ducked my head. "No! I'm just making sure we greet everyone."

"Uh-huh." She didn't seem to buy my excuse.

I busied myself wiping a spotless section of the counter, hoping she wouldn't push the issue, but it didn't do any good.

Marcy's voice softened. "Was it one of the Rogues?"

I mumbled something unintelligible and prayed the floor would open up and swallow me whole.

"Aw, don't be embarrassed." She bumped my shoulder lightly. "You wouldn't be the first girl to get a little tongue-tied around those guys."

"It's not—" I started, but that was as far as I got before she started laughing.

"Relax, Sadie. I won't tease you. Not too much, anyway," she promised, straightening up and giving me a wink. "Besides, if it was who I think it was...you have good taste."

I made a noncommittal noise and focused hard on reorganizing the napkin dispenser.

Marcy let it go, thankfully, and we settled into the steady rhythm of the early afternoon rush. But every time the door jingled, my heart leaped all over again.

Only it was never him.

By the time the lunch crowd thinned, I told myself it was better this way. Hunter had probably forgotten all about me, and I needed to do the same.

Even if my heart wasn't quite ready to listen.

By closing time, all of the pastries were gone, and the smell of fresh bread had faded into a faint, comforting warmth that clung to the walls. Marcy was cleaning the mixers in the back while I wiped down the empty tables and flipped the chairs upside down on top of them.

Once that was done, I walked into the kitchen. "Need help with anything else before I go?"

"Can you mop the floor in the walk-in?" she asked. "I did it earlier after dropping a couple of eggs, but I figure it's better to be safe than sorry when it comes to cleanliness."

"Definitely," I agreed with a nod.

I was fine until I stepped into the walk-in. Although it was big as far as fridges went, it felt small when the door shut behind me. I didn't like tight spaces, but I took a steadying breath and shook off my anxiety as best I could.

Still, my pulse kicked a little faster, the way it always did when rooms started to feel too closed in. I finished mopping as quickly as I could, telling myself it was silly to get worked up over nothing, heaving a deep sigh of relief when I finally escaped the fridge and joined Marcy in the kitchen again.

Not wanting her to notice I was feeling a little off, I grabbed a bag from behind the counter and tied it off, then called, "I'm taking out the trash."

"Thanks!" Marcy's voice floated from the kitchen.

I forced a smile and made my way to the side exit, pushing open the heavy door with my hip. The cool evening air rushed over my skin, chasing away the tight feeling in my chest.

I tossed the bag into the dumpster and wiped my hands on my apron. As I turned to head back inside, something glinted out of the corner of my eye. Frowning, I stepped closer to the window.

A jagged crack snaked its way from the bottom left corner to the center of the glass. It was too big not to notice, which meant that it hadn't been there this morning.

Biting my lip, I leaned in a little, peering through the damaged pane. Nothing looked disturbed in the office. No broken glass on the floor. No sign anyone had tried to get in.

Still, unease curled low in my belly.

Heading into the kitchen, I let Marcy know what I'd found. We padded into the office, and she peered through the broken glass like I'd just done from the outside.

Shrugging, she murmured, "Probably just a truck that kicked up a rock from the parking lot. I'll call Austin."

4

HUNTER

Viper and I had pushed the limits to finish the run as fast as humanly possible. But short of sprouting wings and outrunning the devil himself, we could only ride so damn fast. Two full days on the road, and by the time I'd rolled into the compound, briefed Fox, and grabbed a shower, the bakery had already closed.

I'd tried to sleep but kept waking up soaked in sweat and hard enough to pound nails. After three hours of tossing and cursing, I finally gave up.

Spending ten minutes under an ice-cold spray helped ease the ache in my cock but did nothing for the one in my chest. I'd been shocked at how much I missed her.

I quickly toweled off, padded into the bedroom, checked the clock, and groaned.

Some bakeries opened at the crack of dawn. Not this one. Because the universe liked fucking with me, Country Crust didn't open its doors until seven.

Which meant I had time to kill. And no patience left to kill it with.

For a second, I considered grabbing my SUV and parking across the street like some unhinged stalker, but if Sadie or her boss saw me, I'd have to come up with a reason to be there. One that didn't include the words *I haven't stopped thinking about your mouth in two fucking days*. It was too early to reveal my level of obsession with Sadie.

I needed to go for a ride.

After throwing on black jeans, a gray T-shirt, and my cut, I sat on the edge of the bed to lace up my boots. Once that was done, I grabbed my keys, wallet, and phone, then headed out to my bike.

June in Tennessee could get hot as hell, but at this hour, it was spring-soft. A cool breeze ruffled my hair as I swung a leg over the bike, then put on my helmet. As I approached the gate, I nodded to the prospect on duty before peeling off down the road.

I took a side route with lots of trees and open

fields, less houses, and no traffic. Just the rumble of my engine, the wind in my ears, and the blur of green flashing by in my periphery.

The forty-minute loop cleared most of the clutter from my head, but the second I turned toward town, she was back in my thoughts like she never left.

Sweet, sunshiny Sadie Morgan, with her gorgeous blue eyes and her shy smile that wrecked the fuck out of me.

I glanced at my watch. Six thirty. *Son of a bitch.* Still thirty fucking minutes.

Figuring I'd just do a drive-by, I headed toward the bakery. Maybe park up the road and find a place to wait without being seen.

It turned out I didn't need to because she was already outside.

Sadie stood near the side door, talking to some guy who looked like he'd stepped off the cover of a fucking Barbie catalog. Neatly cut blond hair, clean-shaven, and a boy-next-door smile. And young. Probably only a few years older than Sadie.

Not that I gave a shit. Our age difference had ceased to matter once she flashed me that shy smile the first day we met.

The Ken-doll said something, making Sadie laugh.

My jaw hardened, and my hands clenched the handlebars. The next thing I knew, I was easing the bike into the alley and cutting the engine ten feet from them.

Both heads turned, and Ken frowned, but Sadie lit up like I'd just stepped out of her favorite daydream.

"Hunter," she said softly, a sweet smile curving her plush lips. Her voice was slightly breathless, and it made me think of sex and my name falling from her lips while she broke apart beneath me.

Fucking hell.

My cock twitched, and every possessive instinct I had roared to the surface.

"Wesley," I said, my voice low and hard.

Her smile faltered. "What?"

"My name," I told her, watching those pretty brows draw together. "It's Wesley, sunshine."

Her lips parted. "But I thought..."

Her hands fluttered nervously at her sides.

"You call me Wesley," I said, dismounting and prowling toward her. My boots hit the pavement with slow, deliberate steps until I stood only inches away from them.

I reached out and slid my fingers into her soft brown hair, letting the strands slip through my fingers. Her breath caught, and all I could think was...*mine.*

A throat cleared behind me, and I turned my head slowly, pinning the Ken doll with a look that had ended conversations. And lives.

He shifted his weight like he wanted to run but thought better of it. Then he swallowed hard and straightened his shoulders, trying not to look intimidated.

"We were talking," he snapped.

Ballsy.

But still a dumbass.

Nobody spoke to an Iron Rogue without respect. And a healthy amount of fear.

I arched a brow but didn't say a word. I didn't have to, not when the threat in my silence said everything. He was staring into the eyes of a ruthless predator, and he knew it.

He paled and shifted back a step. Not much, but enough.

So he has some survival instinct buried under all that stupid.

"Go," I said flatly.

He hesitated, glancing at Sadie.

I growled and took a menacing step forward,

seconds away from using my fist to rearrange his face.

Sadie's hand landed on my arm, warm and light, and my focus snapped back to her.

She looked up at me with wide eyes.

"Wait. Austin is fixing the window," she explained, motioning to the cracked pane near the door.

"What happened?" I asked, my frown deepening as I looked at the glass. A jagged crack sliced through the center and down to the corner.

Sadie shrugged, but her fingers fidgeted slightly against her apron.

"Probably a rock," she said too quickly. "No big deal."

I didn't answer.

Maybe it was a rock.

But it had hit dead center. Too clean. Too precise.

The window was old and thick, probably original to the building, and that was the only reason it hadn't shattered. If it had been modern, the glass would've blown out completely.

And the way she said it... as though she was trying to convince herself.

My gut twisted, low and hard, and I'd learned a long time ago not to ignore that feeling.

But the extra tension crawling under my skin had a different source—and he was standing right next to her.

I let the kid finish the job, but I didn't like it. Not the way he stood too close or kept trying to catch Sadie's eye and engage her in conversation.

Annoyed as fuck, I crossed my arms and watched him sweat as he replaced the pane under my heavy stare.

Sadie stayed close but quiet. Every time he lifted his voice to ask a question or made a sudden movement, she shifted closer to me. Just barely. You wouldn't notice if you weren't trained to see it.

But I saw it and loved knowing she already felt safe with me.

By the time the kid packed up and left—without saying a word to me, a smart move—I was already calculating the angles on the building, itching to put up a camera and a better security system.

Just as I finished scanning the perimeter again, the bakery door swung open and Marcy stepped out, wiping her hands on a towel and grinning like she already knew what I was doing.

I'd met her when she'd signed the lease for the

bakery, and my assessment of her had been positive. She was easygoing but sharp. The kind of woman who saw more than she let on and was highly amused when people assumed that her jovial disposition meant she was a little airheaded.

"Something wrong, or are you just looking for an excuse to hang around?" she asked, her eyes dancing as she glanced between me and Sadie.

I pointed at the window. "A broken window, no cameras, and a basic alarm. That's not gonna cut it."

Marcy followed my gaze, then shrugged. "We didn't have any issues during the buildout or while I was gearing up for the opening."

"Doesn't mean you won't now."

Her smile faded just a touch. She knew I wasn't playing games.

"Fair enough." She nodded slowly, and then her grin came right back. "So...are you offering to fix that because this is Iron Rogue's property, making it club business? Or because a certain someone makes cookies and blushes like a Disney princess?"

I didn't answer.

Marcy laughed. "Thought so."

I leveled a look at her. "We take care of what's ours. Something happens in Iron Rogues' territory, we handle it before it becomes a problem."

That part was true.

But it wasn't the real reason I was here. I took care of what was mine.

Marcy didn't argue. She didn't look surprised, either.

Her gaze landed on Sadie—who was practically pressed up against my side—and then back at me.

"You gonna do it now, or do you want me to pretend you're not already planning to stay all morning?"

"Already on it," I said, pulling out my phone. I called one of our officers, Midnight, who co-owned Iron Shield, our private security company, and told him what I needed. He didn't ask questions, which was typical since he had a similar background to mine. Though he'd been a SEAL.

"Be there in fifteen," he grunted.

True to his word, Midnight rolled in fast, his SUV loaded with gear. As he unloaded it, he offered his help.

"Got it handled," I replied.

He handed over the equipment with a nod, then turned to leave, pausing when he spotted my girl. A barely there smirk formed on his mouth, like he suddenly understood why I wanted to do the job myself.

"You're so fucked when the guys hear about this," he gibed, his smirk growing.

He wasn't wrong. I'd given my brothers plenty of shit when they'd found their old ladies. I was sure they'd use every opportunity to return the favor.

"Fuck off," I grunted.

He laughed as he climbed back into his SUV before repeating, "So fucked." Then he was gone.

Marcy disappeared back inside after a minute, trusting me to take care of this.

"I guess I'd better get back to work," Sadie said reluctantly as she trudged toward the door.

"Go work, sunshine. Let you know when I'm done."

"Okay," she replied softly, giving me a sweet smile before following her boss.

I installed the camera they were expecting—just one, right above the entrance. It covered the sidewalk, the parking lot, and part of the road.

Then I added three more. One angled toward the back door. One near the alley. And the last one—smaller and more discreet—just inside, tucked in the upper corner of the front window.

They were all connected to my phone, feeding into an app I controlled. Now I'd be able to see Sadie anytime she was at work.

She wandered back out just as I was putting my tools back into a bag Midnight had brought with the supplies.

"You really didn't have to do this." Her voice carried the same sugary warmth that had wrecked me in the first place. "I mean...we're just a bakery, not exactly a target for robberies or anything like that."

I looked at her. Really looked. And nearly smiled when she squirmed and red stained her cheeks.

"You're not *just* anything," I told her. My voice came out rougher than I meant it to, but I didn't bother hiding the hunger and possession I was plagued with.

She blinked, her blue eyes a little hazy and lips parted slightly.

The desire to bite her plush bottom lip was riding me hard, and I had to cough to cover my groan.

I put my hand out and muttered, "Your phone."

She dug it out of the front pocket of her apron and placed it in my open palm. I quickly added my contact information, then gave it back.

"Anything else happens, you call me," I instructed. "No matter how small you think it might be."

"Thank you," she whispered, her fingers brushing mine as she took back her cell. She was so fucking soft. And warm. It felt like just touching her gave me a fever.

Pink bloomed on her cheeks, and she chewed her bottom lip for a moment before asking, "Do you want mine too?"

"Already have it, sunshine," I admitted gruffly. It was time I started easing her into her future.

To my astonishment, she didn't look scared. She also didn't ask how, and I didn't volunteer the information.

Then she tucked a loose strand of hair behind her ear before placing her hand on my biceps and using it for balance as she went up on her toes to brush a kiss over my cheek.

"I hope I see you again soon," she whispered.

"Count on it, sunshine," I replied, smiling when she blushed again.

Then she was gone. And I was left feeling cold... bereft. As if I'd lost something precious. I opened the app on my phone and watched her helping customers at the counter for way longer than I should have.

But the window was still nagging at me, triggering my protective instincts.

Sadie was bright and happy, but while most people wouldn't notice, I knew she was breakable.

And there wasn't a chance in hell I'd let anything —or anyone—ever come close to trying.

Sadie wasn't just soft.

She wasn't just sweet.

She was mine.

5

SADIE

The bakery smelled like my own personal heaven of warm sugar, fresh bread, and a hint of cinnamon lingering in the air, but none of the delicious pastries tempted me. My stomach was too busy being tied up in a thousand nervous knots, which was ridiculous.

I just saw Wesley yesterday, so the odds of him coming in again this morning were probably slim. If he hadn't been so quick to install that temporary security camera the other day, I'd know for sure that he'd be back soon. Instead, I spent the next two days watching for him. I hadn't been disappointed yesterday, but I doubted he would come by every day.

Even knowing that, I rearranged the already perfectly organized pastry trays as though he'd even

notice. Assuming he came in...which he wasn't going
to do.

Marcy caught me smoothing my apron for the
third time and laughed. "Young love."

I rolled my eyes and muttered, "You're not that
much older than me."

It was easier to point that out than to think about
the fact that I didn't even really know Wesley, no
matter how attracted I was to him.

"I have almost an entire decade on you."

I rolled my eyes and teased, "Then you look good
for your age."

"Whatever," she huffed, tossing the towel she'd
been drying her hands on at me. "But take it from
me...love keeps you young. So don't even bother
trying to resist when Hunter tells you that he's taking
you on a date. Just go for it."

There was a lot to take in with what she'd just
said, so I started with what felt like the most obvious
to me. "I think you meant when he *asks* me out
instead of tells me, not that it's going to happen
either way."

"That's what I thought when I met Derek
during my sophomore year of high school." Her
smile turned dreamy. "He was the star quarterback,
and I was the girl who spent all of her time in the

kitchen baking. I had no clue that he even knew I was alive until he came right up to me in the hallway between classes and told me that he was taking me to prom."

My heart melted at her story. "Aw, that's so sweet."

"I love Derek with all my heart, but I have to admit that when Hunter does the telling thing with you, it's gonna be a heck of a lot hotter." Marcy wagged her brows. "My guy was just a boy back then, but yours is all man."

"Wesley isn't mine," I protested, my cheeks heating.

She shot me a knowing look at my use of his first name. "I am so going to enjoy him proving you wrong."

The bell over the door jingled, and I whipped around, nearly knocking over a tray of lemon bars... only to find a little old lady shuffling in with a walker.

I let out a shaky breath and pasted on a smile, grateful my face was already red from the ovens.

"Welcome to Country Crust," I chirped before helping her pick out a few pastries.

The morning rush picked up from there, giving me just enough to do to keep my mind occupied.

Mostly. But every time the door chimed, my traitorous heart reacted the same way.

Finally, I was sliding a tray of cinnamon rolls into the display when the bell jingled again.

I didn't look right away. I was determined to act normal and professional. But then I felt a shift in the air.

Slowly, I turned. And there he was. The sexy biker who I hadn't been able to get off my mind.

The wind had ruffled his thick black hair, and his beard looked even scruffier than yesterday. His sharp amber eyes zeroed in on me with laser focus, and my heart forgot how to beat.

He prowled toward the counter, and I dropped the pastry tongs with a loud clatter, fumbling to catch them as they bounced off the edge of the display case.

Wesley's mouth twitched. The curve of his lips wasn't quite a smile, but it was close enough for butterflies to swirl in my belly.

"Morning, sunshine," he rumbled, voice like rough gravel.

"Wesley."

I'd been dreaming about this moment all day, but his name was all I could get out.

He stopped in front of the counter, those golden

eyes scanning the pastry case like he was sizing up a threat.

"Coffee," he said, voice low and gravelly.

I nodded quickly and grabbed a cup, feeling his gaze on me the whole time. My hands shook just enough that I almost dropped the lid, but I managed to snap it on without incident. When I slid the cup across the counter to him, I blurted, "You should get a cookie, too."

Wesley quirked a brow.

"On the house," I added hastily, feeling my cheeks heat. "You know...for helping out with our security system."

"You wanna pick one out for me, I'll eat it."

I scrambled to grab a wax paper bag and dropped a double chocolate chip cookie inside. It was still warm from the oven because Marcy had just made another batch since they'd turned out to be a bestseller.

Wesley handed me a crumpled five-dollar bill, his big fingers brushing mine in the exchange. The brief contact sent a jolt up my arm, and I dropped the cash.

Proving he was as observant as I thought—and had incredible reflexes—he caught the money and pressed it back into my hand.

"Thanks."

His gaze lingered on my face for a beat, and then he nodded once before turning to go.

He paused when the bell over the door jingled, and Austin strolled inside, his gaze immediately searching me out. Hunter faced away from me so I couldn't see his expression, but when Austin finally noticed him staring, he paled a little. After a second, Hunter's head twisted around, and his eyes were filled with heat, making goose bumps break out over my skin. Then he looked at Austin one more time before moving toward the exit again.

I watched him walk out, the bell over the door jingling softly behind him.

Only after he disappeared down the street did I realize I was still standing there, clutching the five-dollar bill like a lifeline. And grinning like a lovesick fool.

I worked on autopilot when Austin ordered a muffin and barely processed his attempts to start a conversation. When he left, I pulled the bill from where I'd stuffed it in my pocket and stared at it dreamily.

Thank goodness Marcy was also an amateur matchmaker because, after watching the entire inter-action, she didn't chastise me for being such a hot mess around Wesley. Instead, she shot me a triumphant grin and singsonged, "Told you so."

Not even her boast could pop my bubble. I floated through the rest of the afternoon in a haze of happiness, replaying every second of Wesley's visit in my head. By the time the clock hit closing, I practically hummed as I stacked the chairs. Marcy was counting out the register, humming along to the oldies station we always kept playing low in the background.

"I'll check the mailbox before I head out," I called, grabbing my bag from the office.

"Thanks, hon!" Marcy replied, not looking up.

The small metal box was mounted on the wall just outside the front door. I twisted the knob and pulled it open, expecting nothing more exciting than a flyer or two. Instead, a folded sheet of paper sat inside.

My brows drew together when I lifted it out and noticed nothing was written on the outside.

Even though the street was empty, I glanced around before I flipped it open.

Stay away from them.

That was it. I had no idea what the message

meant. Or who wrote it since there wasn't a signature at the bottom.

My heart started to pound, hard and fast.

I read the words again as if they might rearrange themselves into something less scary, but it didn't help. I still didn't know who "them" was. Although, if I had to guess, they were probably referring to the Iron Rogues since I hadn't really met anyone else recently who could be described in the plural like that.

I twisted the paper in my hands, torn between running back inside to Marcy and pulling out my phone to text Wesley.

He'd already done so much, and Country Crust was her baby. Plus, she was my boss.

My fingers hovered over my phone, uncertainty rooting me to the sidewalk. Then it buzzed in my hand.

A new text lit up the screen.

WESLEY

Checking in.

I had no explanation for how he'd known the perfect time to send me a message. But Marcy didn't seem the least bit surprised when she came out to see what was taking me so long with the mail.

Marcy's eyes dropped to the phone still clutched in my hand, then the note dangling from my other fingers. She didn't even blink.

"I told you Hunter would watch out for you." Her voice teased, but her eyes were serious. "Hiring you was the best decision I've made since opening the bakery, and not just because you're amazing."

"You don't think he somehow knows about this already, do you?" I glanced at the screen of my phone again. "It has to be a coincidence, right?"

"I recommend going with whichever theory makes you feel better." She patted me on the shoulder. "But also, get ready to see him again soon. I'd be willing to bet my ownership in the bakery that he's on his way here now."

I hoped she was right because I already knew I would be safe with Wesley here.

6

HUNTER

SADIE

There was a weird note in the bakery's mailbox. It's probably just a joke, and I'm overreacting.

As I read the text, my frown deepened, and I fired back a message without hesitation.

ME

Be right there.

"Sadie?" Fox asked, his tone knowing.

I looked up. Apparently, I wasn't as unreadable as I liked to think.

He chuckled. "I recognize that look. See it anytime a brother's old lady is involved in questionable shit."

"Fair point," I muttered. "Something's off at the bakery. I don't know what yet, but it's not nothing."

Fox jerked his chin toward the door. "Go. We'll finish this later."

I nodded and was already moving, stalking out of his office and straight to my bike.

Watching Sadie on the cameras had forced me to slow down a little. She was soft, skittish, and if I pushed too hard, she might run. Not that she'd get far—she was mine. Always would be. And if it came down to it, I'd chase her ass down, tie her to the bed, and take my time proving it.

I'd also been keeping an eye out for shady shit. So far, nothing. That made the tension that coiled in my chest when I saw her anxious expression as she read a note outside the shop hit harder than I expected.

When I pulled up, Sadie and Marcy were sitting at one of the bakery's tiny café tables inside, both heads turning at the sound of my engine. Marcy said something that made Sadie blush like crazy, and if I hadn't been half out of my mind with worry and fury, I might've smiled. She was too sweet for this world, and way too damn sweet for me, but I didn't care. She was mine.

The women stepped outside just as I swung off my bike.

"Hey, sunshine," I greeted her first, then nodded at her boss. "Marcy."

"Thanks for coming," Marcy said as she nudged Sadie, who gave me a soft, shy smile.

As I approached, she held out a plastic bag with a small piece of paper inside.

"Good girl," I praised, one corner of my mouth lifting.

"I wasn't sure it was serious enough to go to the cops, so I didn't want to ruin any prints."

Marcy snorted but didn't say a word.

"The Iron Rogues will handle it," I said, voice low and hard.

"But—"

"They're the authority around here, Sadie," Marcy said with a shrug. No judgment, no hesitation. Just stating a fact. Then she looked at me sideways and smiled. "They take care of their own."

Sadie flushed deeper, peeking up at me through her lashes. It wasn't intentional—she had no idea how naturally seductive she was. And no clue how fucking hard it made me.

"But we're not part of the club," she whispered.

"*I'm* not," Marcy said with a sly grin.

"I thought women couldn't join," Sadie added, brows knitting.

"Not as patches," I said. "As old ladies."

Her sky-blue eyes widened. "That's real? Calling them old ladies? I thought it was just something from movies or books."

Holding her gaze, I grunted. "Claimed women are called old ladies."

"Oh." Her smile turned wistful before she shook her head and stepped back. "Well, I'm, um, not...I mean, I'm not claimed, so you really don't have to—"

"One thing at a time, sunshine," I muttered. It was the wrong time for that conversation. But it would be happening real fucking soon.

I flipped the note over and read the words. Fury instantly whipped through me. Sharp. Blinding. Someone had threatened my girl.

"It could be for me," Marcy offered, but she didn't sound convinced.

"'Them,'" I muttered, eyes still on the paper. My jaw clenched, and I raised my gaze to her face. "Piss anyone off? You or Derek?"

"No one I can think of," she said, eyes narrowing.

I was sure it was meant for Sadie. And "them" referred to my club. Maybe it was just some loser with a crush and no balls. Or perhaps it was worse.

I dug my phone from my pocket and called my prez.

"Fox," he answered.

"Got a problem," I said, then gave him a quick rundown about the window and now the note.

"You install cameras?"

"Yeah."

"How many?"

"More than one." I didn't know if Marcy or Sadie were aware of just how many I'd planted, so I was vague in answering.

"Figured. Send Deviant the app login. He'll start pulling footage."

Deviant, besides being an enforcer, was a fucking tech genius. If there was something on the video, he'd find it.

"Will do. Sadie bagged the note. I'll drop it at Iron Shield so Midnight can run the paper for prints."

"Good girl," Fox muttered, impressed.

I growled, and he chuckled. "Now who's whipped?"

Muttering an expletive, I hung up.

Turning back to Sadie, I locked eyes with her. "Gonna figure this out."

Marcy cleared her throat and smiled. "Well, I'll

lock up and get out of your hair. You'll take care of Sadie, yeah?"

"Damn straight," I said, winking at my girl. The heat in my eyes hinted at the double meaning, and I smirked when her cheeks turned rosy.

"See you tomorrow," Marcy called as she disappeared back inside, giggling.

"Thank you," Sadie murmured softly. "We appreciate your help."

"Don't have to thank me, sunshine. I take care of what's mine."

She tilted her head slightly, biting her lip. Hope flickered across her face, soft and unsure. "But...I'm not yours."

"Wrong," I said, my voice firm and final. "You've been mine since the moment I laid eyes on you."

"Really?" she breathed, cheeks flushing.

I nodded as the color crawled down her throat and disappeared into her shirt. I couldn't help but wonder how far it went. Would her skin turn that same pink when I made her come? When I left my handprint on her ass?

I clenched my jaw, forcing the images out of my head before I exploded in my jeans like a horny teenager.

"Yours to...protect?" Sadie asked, her voice tentative, peering up through her dark lashes again.

I reached out and pressed a hand gently to her stomach, guiding her back until she hit the brick wall beside the bakery window. Dropping my head, I leaned in until my lips brushed the shell of her ear.

"Mine to protect. Mine to touch. Mine to fuck," I murmured, letting my nose glide along her jaw until our lips were just a breath apart. "All of you, sunshine. *Mine.*"

Then I crushed my mouth to hers.

A deep growl rumbled from my chest as my hands settled at her waist, holding her still while I devoured her. She tasted even better than she smelled, and when I ran my tongue along the seam of her lips, she parted for me without hesitation.

"That's it, sunshine," I whispered. "Open for me."

I kissed her deeper, sliding my hands around to cup her ass. She was perfect. Curvy, soft, and made for me.

My hips pressed into her, my cock straining against my jeans, but when she let out a low, breathy moan, I froze.

That sound was for me. *Only me.* If anyone else heard it, I'd lose my shit and kill the motherfucker.

"Wesley?" she whispered, dazed and panting. But when our eyes met, there was a flicker of confusion...and wariness.

"You have no idea how much I want you, sunshine," I rasped, brushing my thumb across her lower lip. "But not here. Anyone hears your pretty little moans, I'll lose my fucking mind."

"Oh," she breathed, then smiled, flushed and pleased.

I pulled back enough to cool down but kept hold of her hand. "Be ready, sunshine. Eventually, we're gonna finish what we started. And I'm not stopping until you're begging me to."

7

SADIE

I was trembling from Wesley's words but couldn't think of a response, so I reluctantly blurted, "I guess I'll head home."

Wesley's amber eyes locked onto mine—sharp and clear while I was still foggy from our kiss. "You're not driving yourself."

His tone—low, gruff, and completely unmovable —sent a shiver down my spine.

"I live with my parents," I blurted, my cheeks filling with heat at the confession.

Hunter didn't react except to say, "Get your stuff. I'm taking you."

A part of me wanted to tell him that wasn't necessary, but it was drowned out by the side still rattled from the creepy note, so I just nodded. And if

I was being brutally honest with myself, I just wanted to be around him as long as possible.

Without another word, he slipped my bag off my shoulder and guided me toward the door with a hand on the small of my back.

Somehow, by the time we got outside, he had the keys to my car dangling from his fingers. Still too stunned to argue, I climbed into the passenger side and pressed the back of my head against the rest, squeezing my eyes shut as he slid into the driver's seat.

The bakery disappeared behind us as Hunter pulled onto the main drive, his focus on the road. It wasn't until we hit the town limits that my brain caught up with what was happening.

"You're driving my car," I stated the obvious.

"Yeah."

"What about your bike?"

Hunter didn't look worried. "It'll be safe at the bakery for now, and someone from the club can come get me later."

"Oh."

I settled back into my seat, feeling silly for worrying when he'd already figured it out. Wesley "Hunter" Hastings didn't seem like a man who left things to chance.

I twisted my hands together in my lap, sneaking glances at him when I thought he wouldn't notice. His jaw was tight, a muscle ticking near his beard. Knowing he was so angry on my behalf made me feel better about the situation.

When we pulled into my neighborhood, Hunter's gaze sharpened, taking in every detail.

"This one?" he asked when I pointed at my parents' house.

"Yeah."

He parked in the driveway, and I climbed out of the car and followed him up the front porch steps. After he handed me my keys, I unlocked the door.

He followed me inside, shutting the door behind us with a heavy finality that echoed through the quiet. His eyes swept the living room, then landed back on me. "When will your parents be home?"

I winced. "They're on a road trip in their new RV to celebrate my dad's retirement."

Wesley's expression darkened. "So you're alone."

I swallowed hard. "Yeah, but it's not that big of a deal—"

"It is to me."

His fiercely spoken words knocked the breath from my lungs. Deep down, a secret part of me had wanted a guy who worried about me. Who wanted to protect me as though I mattered to them. Probably because that was how my dad was with my mom.

He didn't give me time to reply. "You're not staying here by yourself."

"I'm not?" I asked, my eyes widening.

He jerked his chin toward the hallway. "Pack a bag."

I gawked at him, unsure how to respond.

"I meant what I said, sunshine," he added, softer but no less intense. "You're mine. I'm not gonna let anything happen to you."

The possessiveness in his voice had those pesky butterflies swirling in my belly again. So I just nodded before turning to hurry to my bedroom, my pulse hammering in my ears.

I didn't realize that he had followed me until I dragged a suitcase out of my closet and turned around, bumping against his broad chest. His strong hands gripped my waist, and I tilted my head back to stare up at him. "Oops, sorry."

"Crash into me whenever you want, sunshine." His amber eyes filled with heat, the color darkening to an almost molten brown. "Gives me an excuse to get you in my arms."

I shook my head with a giggle. "After that kiss, I'm surprised you think you need one."

"Glad to hear that." His lips curved into a smirk as he dipped his head. "'Cause I don't want to pretend that's not exactly where I want you to be all the damn time."

His mouth covered mine, and my suitcase crashed to the floor at my side as I lifted my arms to twine them around his neck. Our tongues tangled together in a deep kiss that left me breathless and wanting more...something that Wesley gave me before I could even ask for it.

He used his grip on my waist to carry me over to the narrow bed, where he laid me down. Then he levered his powerful body over mine, careful not to press me too hard into the mattress.

I gasped when I felt the hard bulge in his jeans, but he stopped and gazed down at me with worry.

"This triggering your claustrophobia?" he asked.

I melted at his thoughtfulness, not surprised that he'd picked up on it, considering how observant he was.

"Not even a little bit," I rasped.

I should've felt trapped. Pinned down. But my world was narrowed to Wesley. Nothing else mattered. Not even my fear of tight spaces.

His lips captured my mouth in another passionate kiss, and it wasn't long before we were both panting for breath. "Fuck, sunshine. Didn't bring you home to fuck you. Just wanted to make sure you were safe."

He had just given me the perfect opportunity to put the brakes on what we were doing before things spiraled even more. I had only met him four days ago, and we'd spent maybe a grand total of an hour together during that time. Maybe it was leftover adrenaline from the note making me throw my usual caution to the wind.

Whatever the reason, I had no doubts about what I wanted.

Lifting my hand, I stroked his bearded cheek. "I've never felt safer than right here with you."

"You're too fucking tempting. Time to finish what we started," he muttered before claiming my mouth again.

I clutched his shoulders while his teeth nipped at my lips and his tongue slid against mine. As the kiss grew more passionate, his hand drifted to my breast, and his thumb brushed over the pebbled nipple through my shirt. My back arched, pressing it deeper into his palm.

"Like that, sunshine?"

I breathed, "Uh-huh."

"Then you're gonna fucking love this."

He slipped his hand under my shirt, tugging the soft material up over the swell of my breasts. He lowered his head, his breath hot against my bra cup. It was just simple white cotton, but I didn't feel awkward over how unsexy it was because there was no missing the desire in his heated gaze. Then my thoughts scattered when he sucked one of my nipples into his mouth through the material.

"Yesss," I hissed, gripping the back of his head to press his mouth closer to my breast.

His deep chuckle sent goose bumps across my skin. "Only gets better, sunshine."

My back bowed off the mattress so he could slide his hand beneath me to undo the clasp on my bra. I also helped him lift my shirt over my head, leaving me naked from the waist up. My bare skin prickled as his gaze raked over me, heating even more.

"You're so fucking gorgeous."

His compliment—and the masculine approval in his eyes—made me feel as though I was the sexiest woman in the world. But then I remembered how inexperienced I was. And that Wesley deserved to know before this went any further.

Tugging on the hair at the back of his head, I waited until he glanced up at me to whisper, "Um...I should probably tell you that I've never done this before."

"Are you sayin' you're a virgin?"

I nodded. "Yeah."

"Fucking hell." His hand slid down to cup between my legs. "This pussy is gonna be all mine because my sunshine saved it for me like a good girl."

I'd always been one to follow the rules and never make waves—all traits for a good girl. But the way Wesley said the phrase brought a whole new meaning to it. "You're not mad?"

"Hell no." He pressed his palm deeper against my core. "I fucking love knowing that I'm the only man who gets to see, touch, and even taste you like this."

"Taste?" I echoed, my cheeks filling with heat that was more due to passion than embarrassment.

"Already addicted to your lips and pretty nipples." His smile was wicked. "It's a safe bet the same thing'll happen when I get my mouth on your pussy."

My inner walls clenched at the image his words painted. He didn't leave me wondering what it would feel like, moving down my body and quickly removing my jeans and panties. Then he wedged his broad shoulders between my thighs and devoured me as though he was starving. Wesley used his lips, tongue, and teeth to quickly make me come before I even knew it was happening.

"So fucking sweet, sunshine. But I want more."

He started to work a finger inside me, my pussy fighting him every step of the way until he swirled his tongue around my clit. My hips jerked up, sending him knuckle-deep inside me. The slight pinch of pain sent me flying over the edge again.

"Yes, oh yes, Wesley!" I cried, my head thrashing against the pillow as fireworks burst behind my eyelids.

My wits were scattered from two mind-blowing orgasms, but I still managed to blink my eyes open and focus on Wesley as he stripped for me. My eyes widened when he slid his zipper down to free his cock. I knew it was cliché, but that didn't stop me from blurting, "I don't think you're going to fit."

He smirked as he climbed back on top of me. "Trust me, sunshine. Your sweet pussy is gonna wrap around my cock like it was made for me."

His confidence eased my concerns, which turned out to be a good thing because my muscles weren't tense when he kneeled between my legs. He gripped my hips, his eyes burning into mine as he punched his hips forward and filled me in one hard thrust.

I let out a startled yelp, and he stroked his hand up and down my side.

"Sorry, sunshine. Figured it was better to get the hard part over fast before you had the chance to worry about how much it was gonna hurt."

I wiggled my hips and winced a little. "It's not that bad."

"Maybe this'll help." With his dick anchored inside me, he covered my body and claimed my mouth in a deep kiss.

When he finally lifted his head, the pain was only a memory. "It sure did."

"Better now?"

I wiggled my hips again and only felt intense pleasure. "Fantastic."

"Thank fuck," he grunted. "Not sure I can hold back much longer. Your pussy feels so fucking good, clamped around my cock like a vise."

"Then don't," I urged. "I'm ready for more now."

"That's my good girl." He withdrew and plunged back inside, over and over again, until I wasn't sure where I ended and he began. His rhythm was hard and fast, but I managed to keep up.

"I'm so close already," I panted, digging my nails into his shoulders.

"Give it to me, sunshine. Need your pussy to

milk my cock, then I'm gonna come too," he demanded in a hoarse tone.

He wedged his arm between our bodies, his thumb circling my clit until my body went taut and another orgasm rolled over me. "Yes! Wesley, yes!"

"Fuck, yes," he groaned, thrusting into me a few more times before his body shook. "You're mine now, sunshine."

The splash of his hot come against my inner walls sparked another mini-release, and I was barely able to see straight when he rolled onto his back so that I was sprawled on top of him. Between all the orgasms and his possessive words, I was already in deep with Wesley.

8

HUNTER

Sadie sighed, and my still half-hard dick twitched. I was tempted not to let her rest before taking her again. And again. And again.

But I'd just popped her cherry, and her sweet little pussy needed a break before I stretched it with my big cock again.

Twin beds weren't made for a guy my size, either. Since I planned to keep her there for a while, we needed to get back to the clubhouse. She belonged in my space, in my giant bed, wrapped up in my arms with my come leaking out of her, my baby in her belly, and my ring on her finger.

One thing at a time, I reminded myself wryly.

"Let's get you packed, sunshine," I rumbled. "Might make it back in time for food."

"Food?" she echoed, lifting her head and resting her chin on my chest.

"Some of the old ladies take turns making dinner. The boys handle the rest. Except Midnight and Racer—those jackasses aren't allowed anywhere near the kitchen unless it's mealtime."

Sadie giggled, and damn if the sound didn't make something warm spread through my chest.

"Let's go." I gave her ass a light smack and lifted her off my cock with a groan. She mewled in protest, and I squeezed my eyes shut, breathing through the ache. "Don't make sounds like that, sunshine," I gritted out. "If I lose my shit and fuck you again, you won't be able to walk tomorrow."

She smirked, smug and satisfied, and I had to remind myself that breaking her was not the goal. *Not yet.*

"Be a good girl," I warned. "Want that tight little pussy healed up fast 'cause I'm gonna spend a lot of time buried inside it."

That earned me another giggle, followed by the cutest fucking pout that had me shaking my head. I rolled out of bed, grabbed the bag she'd dropped on the floor, and tossed it onto the mattress. She scooted to the other side and stood, glancing back over her shoulder as she crossed the room with an extra swing in her hips that had my dick pulsing again.

I narrowed my eyes. "Behave. If you keep that up, you're gonna earn yourself a spanking."

When she looked interested, I groaned and turned away from temptation. I dressed in record time and nearly sagged in relief when I saw her heading to the bathroom fully clothed.

While she packed her makeup and shampoo or whatever the fuck she needed, I hit her dresser. I grabbed an armful of underwear and dropped it in the suitcase, then the drawer full of shirts. When that was done, I scowled. The bag was already full, and we hadn't even touched her closet.

I wanted to bring as much of her stuff as possible, so there wouldn't be much to retrieve when she realized she'd moved in with me.

I stalked to the closet and found a bigger suitcase and a duffel. Exactly what I needed. By the time Sadie came out of the bathroom, I'd filled and zipped all three. They were lined up by the door, ready to go.

She blinked, glanced at the bags, then back at me with a raised brow.

"Don't know how long this shit's gonna take," I

explained with a shrug. "Figured it's better to have what you need. Don't wanna keep drivin' out here every time you forget a hair tie."

I didn't mention she'd be needing all of it anyway. This wasn't temporary. She just didn't know it yet.

"Oh." She nodded easily and didn't question my explanation. Just trusted me. My chest tightened, pride hitting low and deep. She was so fucking perfect for me.

"Got everything else?"

Sadie looked around the room one last time. "Yep. I'm ready."

I loaded her shit into the trunk of that rusty little clunker she called a car, glaring at it with distaste the whole time. It wasn't dangerously unsafe, but the tin can wasn't gonna cut it for my old lady. She needed something safer. More reliable. I made a mental note to handle that soon.

As we pulled out of the driveway, I clocked her twisting her hands in her lap even though her expression was curious and a little excited.

"What's on your mind, sunshine?"

"It's just..." she hesitated, then laughed softly. "I've never lived anywhere else. So it's a little strange

to think about. And now I'll be living with a guy—"
Her voice cut off, and she looked at me with wide
eyes. "Um...not that we're living together. I mean, I
know—I'm not assuming—"

I reached across the console and laid my hand
over hers, giving her a gentle squeeze. "Relax,
sunshine. You're mine, remember? For now, that
means you sleep where I sleep, live where I live.
We'll figure out the rest later."

The tension bled out of her, and she relaxed back
into the seat. I didn't move my hand, and after a few
seconds, she flipped hers palm up and laced our
fingers together.

Even with the bullshit swirling around us and
danger just on the edge of our horizon, I felt more at
peace than I ever had. Only thing better had been
being inside her, knowing no one else ever had and
never would.

We drove in silence. It was comfortable and easy,
like we'd been doing this for years. As though she
was made just for me.

When we reached the compound gates, she
perked up, straightening in her seat and looking
around with curious, bright eyes.

The gate swung open, and as I approached the

guard shack, Phoenix stepped out. I arched a brow and rolled down the window. Patches didn't normally do security duty. It was one of the jobs we farmed out to prospects because it tested their loyalty, determination, quick thinking, and other skills we looked for in new members.

He scowled before I said a word. "Probies weren't available. Was Viper's turn, but the asshole pulled the pregnant old lady card."

"She's two weeks from her due date," I pointed out, barely suppressing a grin.

Phoenix crossed his arms. "Badass bikers turn into fucking pussies the second their old ladies get knocked up."

He wasn't wrong. But as I fully intended to have Sadie bred as soon as possible and knew I would be just as bad as my brothers, I shouldn't give him shit. But fucking with him would be so much more satisfying.

"Tick tock, asshole," I drawled. "Sooner or later, some sweet thing's gonna own your balls—and you'll be beggin' her to squeeze."

Phoenix narrowed his eyes but didn't miss a beat. "If she squeezes hard enough, maybe I won't turn into a whipped bitch like the rest of you."

I smirked and leaned an elbow on the open window, voice low and smug.

"Keep talking, brother. One day, you'll be on your knees and calling it foreplay."

From the passenger seat, Sadie choked on a laugh and turned her face toward the window, pretending to be interested in the pine trees.

Phoenix flipped me off without a word and stalked back into the shack.

I pulled forward, my hand still resting over Sadie's. As we neared the clubhouse, there was a familiar shift in my shoulders as the solitary weight of the outside world slipped off.

After spending one too many years being knocked around by my dad, my mom had signed the paperwork for me to join the Army at seventeen. I was focused, determined, and talented, so I'd become a Ranger in just under twenty months, when I was still eighteen. After serving two years, I was accepted into Ranger school.

I spent five years in elite operations—giving me serious combat and tactical experience that earned me advanced Ranger and sniper roles. After gaining some experience, I'd been assigned to high-level special missions. People didn't often realize that certain roles within the military could be very solitary. Especially snipers. I had to rely on only myself. Which had served me well when I left to join the FBI.

With a highly decorated military career—even though it had only been eight years—I moved up the ladder at lightning speed. The skills and experience I'd gained in the Army set me on the path to become a high-level tracker, sniper, and interrogator—eventually earning a reputation as one of the best in the country. But once more, I'd been working in a job where I spent more time working solo than as part of a team.

I hit my limit when I was thirty-two. After fifteen years of service and some hard lessons about corruption and times when the laws were just flat-out fucking wrong, I needed a change. One that didn't involve following orders, being isolated, or following the letter of the law.

I'd never intended to return to Tennessee. My parents were dead. I had no family, nowhere to live, and no fucking purpose in life.

I'd known Maverick and Fox when we were kids, but I hadn't kept in touch with anyone.

So I was shocked when Maverick reached out to me after I'd been back for a few months. We fell easily into our old friendship, and he'd eventually encouraged me to check out their MC. Thought it would be a good fit for me. I'd balked, opposed to the idea of being caged again.

Ultimately, he talked me into meeting with Fox and seeing the compound.

When I passed through the gate for the first time, that same weight began to lift from my shoulders. By the time I left that night, I understood.

I hadn't realized I'd been struggling to acclimate to a life without structure. I was lonely and too damn tired to have complete control of my life. In the Iron Rogues, I'd found a leader I trusted, who had earned my obedience. And a family—even if they were a pain in the ass sometimes.

Sadie's fingers tightened around mine when she spotted the clubhouse in the distance—two stories of weathered wood and concrete, a garage big enough to hold dozens of bikes in bad weather. Though she couldn't see it, there were also other buildings, like a clinic built in the back. And after Mav's old lady had their little girl, Luna, we'd put in a playground and barbecue area.

Patched bikes lined up out front like a wall of warning. The place wasn't flashy, but it was fortified. It was blood, loyalty, and fire-forged brotherhood. A fortress we'd built together. For ourselves.

And eventually, for the women we couldn't live without.

Sadie sat quietly beside me, but her eyes were wide, taking it all in like she'd just stepped onto another planet. I didn't blame her. For outsiders, the clubhouse could feel like stepping into the lion's den. But this lion didn't want to eat her. I wanted to keep her.

Permanently.

She tracked the bikes lined up outside and landed on a few tattoo-covered men lounging near the garage, talking shit and sipping beers. They lifted chins in greeting when they spotted me. Their eyes glanced over Sadie, then immediately looked away— not out of disrespect, but because they knew better. She might not be wearing my property patch yet, but Sadie was mine. And no man here was stupid enough to test the boundaries that came with that claim.

I parked out front, cut the engine, and glanced at her. "You good?"

She nodded, her attention bouncing around from one thing to the next. "Yeah. Just...it's different."

"It's ours," I corrected, already out of the car where she couldn't hear me, circling around to her side. "And now it's yours too."

I opened the door, and she smiled up at me as I helped her step out. Then I slipped my arm around her waist so no one questioned her place here—they'd know who she was to me. Her body tucked perfectly into mine, soft curves against hard edges. Just like her sweet innocence perfectly brightened my dark, gritty world.

The front door swung open, and Maverick stepped out, a squirming toddler in his arms and a smirk on his face.

"Thought I heard your growl pull in," he grunted, his face deadpan but laughter dancing in his eyes.

I gave him a withering stare, but he ignored it and looked past me to my woman, nodding at her respectfully. "Welcome to the chaos, Sadie."

She gave a small wave, her fingers curling against my side, but she didn't shy away. Brave girl. She was stepping out of her comfort zone, not letting this place, these people, intimidate her. Just another reason she belonged with me.

If she was surprised that he knew who she was, she didn't let on.

Behind Mav, Molly leaned against the door-frame, already bumping her hip into her man's. "She's prettier than you described," she teased.

"I didn't describe her," I muttered, tugging Sadie closer. "Didn't want to share."

That earned a low chuckle from Maverick as he stepped aside to let us in. Inside, the air was thick with the scent of leather, pine, and something savory coming from the kitchen.

The lounge was a large space where people could gather for a party or to just hang out. It had black leather couches, a pool table, a poker table, and several big-screen televisions. It used to be utterly masculine, like a big bachelor pad, and the red leather stools lining the bar had been the only pop of color in the dark room.

But as my brothers claimed their old ladies, feminine touches had shown up here and there, making it more homey. I appreciated it now because they made the place more welcoming, and Sadie would feel more comfortable in this environment.

Laughter echoed around the common room. Old ladies sat curled up next to their men, some tucked into corners, others sprawled out on couches like they'd always belonged here.

My brothers *had* always belonged here, but their women had become a part of the fabric of the Iron Rogues. And now, so would Sadie.

She hesitated for half a second, clearly aware she

was stepping into someone else's world. I leaned down and spoke low in her ear. "You belong here, sunshine. Give 'em a chance, and they'll love you."

Just not as much as I do. Not even fucking close.

The thought hit hard, knocking the air from my lungs for a second. But then it settled—deep and solid, like it had always been there.

I loved the fuck outta her. That wasn't some maybe or someday thing. It was already done. And living without Sadie? That wouldn't be any kind of life at all. More like breathing through a fucking bullet hole.

Her lips parted as we stepped inside, her gaze darting around the room, wide and curious. But not afraid. Not even close.

There was a gleam in her eyes—eager and bright like she'd just stepped into another world and couldn't quite believe it was real. Her reaction made me chuckle under my breath. Hell, she looked like she'd just stepped onto a movie set and couldn't believe what she was seeing.

Maverick passed Luna to Molly, then dropped onto the couch and pulled his old lady onto his lap, circling his arms around her and their daughter in a possessive hold.

At the bar, Dahlia grinned as she watched Fox

try to wrangle his twin toddlers—one squirming on his shoulder, the other dangling from his hand by the back of her shirt like a damn kitten. Deviant and Storm were with their women nearby, while Nevada, Savage, Inferno, and Racer sat at the bar, drinking beer and barking at the baseball game on one of the TVs.

The place was loud, rough around the edges, and filled with the kind of love only men like us knew how to give—fierce, full-throttle, and all-consuming.

I introduced Sadie quickly, keeping her close the entire time with one hand on her hip. It was a lot, and I'd been a little worried with how shy she was. But she handled it like a fucking pro, giving soft smiles and little waves, all while holding tight to my side.

As soon as we were clear, I nudged her toward the stairs, but Fox called out to me before we reached them.

I pressed a kiss on Sadie's temple.

"Give me a minute, sunshine," I murmured, then walked over.

"New shipment of vests came in," he said, his voice low, just for me. "Sheila picked one up today. Should be done this week."

I nodded once, satisfaction settling in low and

hot inside me. When an Iron Rogue found his woman, he didn't fuck around. We didn't "date" or go slow. We claimed. Fast and hard. And we marked them so everyone knew who they belonged to.

Custom vests used to take weeks. Now Fox kept a stash at the clubhouse already half-patched. Sheila, Tank's old lady, handled the embroidery of the names. She'd already be stitching Sadie on the front and my road name across the back.

"Appreciate it," I muttered before jogging back to my girl. Then we climbed the stairs together.

The clubhouse wasn't massive, so we had several apartments above the buildings we owned across Old Bridge where prospects and some patches lived. But this was the heart of the club. Upstairs, brothers who lived on-site had their own rooms with a private bath, and some were even more like one-bedroom apartments. The rest were spare rooms for whoever needed to crash.

When we reached mine, I unlocked the door and pushed it open, tossing her bags into the closet. Then I turned and hauled her into my arms, burying my face in her neck.

"Overwhelmed?"

She let out a soft laugh. "A little. But I really like it here so far."

"Good." I took her mouth in a deep, claiming kiss...just shy of unhinged. By the time I pulled back, she was clinging to me as though she couldn't stand on her own.

I forced myself to loosen my grip. "How about a bath, sunshine?"

"Are you gonna take it with me?" she asked hopefully, blinking up at me with those big, blue eyes.

My groan was pure torture. "Don't tempt me," I growled.

Grabbing her hand, I led her to the bathroom and turned on the hot water.

When I looked back, she stood in the doorway with her bottom lip stuck out in a little pout that was cute as fuck.

I grinned and shook my head. "You can have your wicked way with me as much as you want tomorrow. I promise."

She huffed but didn't argue. I kissed her quickly and bolted before my restraint snapped clean in half. Then I dropped onto the bed and tried not to think about her naked and wet just ten feet away and failing miserably.

When the bathroom door finally opened, I turned my head and felt my heart stop.

She wore one of my shirts. It hung off her shoulders, halfway down her thighs, drowning her small frame. Somehow, that made it even hotter. Seeing her in my clothes had my cock standing at full attention.

Her hair was damp and hung in waves down her back and over her shoulders. Her skin had been scrubbed pink, and her hard little nipples poked through the cotton like a fucking invitation.

Fuuuuuck.

She gave a shy smile and padded across the room, slipping under the covers beside me...then climbed onto my lap.

"Sadie," I growled, the warning low and shaky. I was one second from saying fuck it and burying my throbbing dick inside her.

"I feel achy," she whispered. "Empty."

Son of a bitch.

I shut my eyes, exhaling slowly. When I opened them, I filled my hands with her tits and muttered, "Can't have that, can we?"

I'd give her what she needed. Always.

There was plenty I could do to her without breaking her tight pussy. And I did every fucking one of them. I worked her with my fingers, then my tongue, until she was screaming my name in ecstasy.

Then I jacked off, pumping hard until I spilled across her bare pussy—then pushed some of it inside.

Claimed.

When I finally dragged her into my arms, I smiled to myself.

She was in my bed. My come was leaking out of her. And the rest was coming real soon.

9

SADIE

The first thing I noticed when I woke up was the warmth. It was unlike anything I experienced before...the kind that came from being completely wrapped up in someone else's body.

My lips curved into a grin as I realized that Wesley had kept me close even while he slept. Somehow, it felt even more intimate than everything we'd done yesterday.

I was tucked against his chest, his arms locked tight around me like he had no intention of ever letting go. One of his hands was splayed over my hip, fingers brushing the hem of the oversized T-shirt I'd slipped on before crawling into his bed. The other was under my head, cradling me close, as though he needed to know exactly where I was even in sleep.

I should've felt overwhelmed since the past twenty-four hours had been a whirlwind of emotions, high and low. Wesley's fierce protectiveness and how he looked and touched me as though I was already his had taken my mind off the threatening note.

A soft breath escaped me, and I shifted just slightly, enough to feel the press of his chest against my back and the steady rhythm of his heartbeat. That was when I realized he wasn't asleep.

Wesley's hand slid from my hip to my belly, fingers spreading out possessively. He dipped his head, brushing his nose against the curve of my neck.

"You okay?" he murmured, voice low and rough from sleep.

I nodded. "Just thinking."

His lips grazed my neck. "Hopefully good thoughts, sunshine."

I smiled softly, my chest tightening. "Hard not to when I wake up with you wrapped around me."

"Good. You're gonna get used to it."

I wanted to ask exactly what he meant by that. If the way he'd touched me had the same weight for him as it had me. But I didn't want to ruin this quiet moment by second-guessing what was happening between us.

Instead, I stayed still in his arms, letting myself be held. And hope.

Eventually, I felt Wesley shift behind me, his lips brushing my temple. "Come on. Let's get you some food before the old ladies start smuggling pastries into their diaper bags."

I laughed before I could stop myself. "You make it sound like a war zone."

Wesley grunted, already sitting up and stretching his massive frame like a lion uncurling from a nap. "When you get that many babies and bikers in one place before breakfast, it kinda is."

The smell of coffee and something sweet hit me the moment we stepped out of Wesley's room and into the main common area. Laughter echoed from the kitchen, the kind that came from women who didn't just tolerate each other—they were genuinely friends.

Wesley's hand found the small of my back as we rounded the corner, and I stiffened instinctively. Not because I didn't like his touch—just the opposite. I enjoyed it too much. But walking into a room full of people who already knew each other—who had history—while I looked like I'd just rolled out of bed and was barely holding it together was a whole different kind of nerve-wracking.

Three women gathered around the kitchen table, each with a mug in hand. Two had babies strapped to their chests, and the other was visibly pregnant. So much so that she looked as though she was ready to pop any minute. She was at the end of the table, turned sideways with her feet propped up on another chair.

The first to spot us had light brown hair and hazel eyes. She smiled warmly at me. "Good morning."

The other women glanced up and grinned when they saw Wesley and me standing in the doorway.

"Morning," I whispered, my cheeks filling with heat as they gawked at us.

Wesley steered me toward them. "This is Sadie."

"It's so nice to meet you." The pregnant one gave me a little wave before dropping her hand back on her rounded stomach. "I'm Rhiannon."

"Oh, I should've introduced myself. Sorry, but Porter is still keeping us up most of the night, so I'm not firing on all cylinders yet." The woman who first spotted me stroked her son's cheek with a sigh. "I'm Ellery."

"And I'm Marnie," the last woman added. "Also sleep deprived thanks to Hank."

"They're such cute reasons to be up all night,

though." I grinned at her son, who gave me a gummy smile.

Marnie's grin widened. "I think you just volunteered yourself for babysitting duty."

"Really?" I gasped. "I'm definitely up for it when I'm not working at the bakery because I love kids, but you barely know me."

"You're with Hunter. That's all I need to know," she replied.

"Same," Ellery echoed.

Rhiannon patted her belly. "I'll definitely take all the help I can get."

Three men joined us in the kitchen, all clearly Iron Rogues members based on their vests. One of them was holding the most adorable little girl who looked to be about a year and a half old. Her eyes were sleepy as she tucked her face against his broad chest.

A guy who looked slightly familiar, with a patch on his leather that named him Viper made a beeline for Rhiannon as I remembered that he'd been with Wesley the day we first met. "You need anything, gorgeous?"

She tilted her head back to smile at him. "Nope, I'm good."

His eyes narrowed as he glanced at the mug in her hand. "What're you drinking?"

"Don't worry. It's herbal tea." She heaved a deep sigh. "I didn't try to sneak in some coffee while you were busy."

He set his hand on top of hers over her belly. "That's my good girl."

His praise sounded so much like Wesley had yesterday when he'd called me a good girl that I shivered remembering it. Luckily, he was the only one who noticed since the other two men strode toward their women to ask similar questions.

After they got the same answers, Wesley murmured, "You want some coffee?"

"Get it while you still can," Marnie suggested.

The tall, tattooed man behind her chuckled, making me blush harder.

"Knock it off, Ice," Wesley growled before guiding me over to a chair.

"Guess we can save giving you shit for another time," the man holding the little girl muttered.

Wesley shook his head and shot him a dry look. "Thanks for the favor, Whiskey."

His club brother smirked. "Anything for you, man."

The easy camaraderie between them all settled something in my chest. But it was still a lot to get used to. A new place and people, so I stuck close to Wesley for the first few minutes, helping where I could and mostly trying not to fidget.

When Ellery offered to let me hold Porter while she ate the plate of pancakes Whiskey brought her, I jumped at the chance. He was soft and warm, smelling faintly of baby shampoo. I cuddled him close and made a silly face that had him cooing up at me.

I didn't realize how quiet it had gotten until I looked up and saw Wesley watching me. His eyes burned with something I didn't know how to name, but it made my breath catch in my chest.

I didn't know if it was wishful thinking, but I swore I saw some possessiveness mixed with hunger in his amber orbs.

It was almost enough to distract me from the fact that he hadn't used protection when we had sex. I hadn't really thought about it until now, while we were surrounded by his club brothers, their wives, and babies. Definitely not the right time to bring it up.

I watched as Whiskey brushed a kiss across

Ellery's temple while she fed their little girl bites of pancake. His arm was draped over the back of their daughter's chair, his hand resting on his wife's shoulder with casual, easy affection. Marnie leaned into Ice's side, and even with a baby strapped to her chest and spit-up on her shoulder, he looked at her like she hung the moon. Viper's position next to Rhiannon was much the same, except his hand still rested on her pregnant belly.

They were all big, tough men. Bikers who were part of a motorcycle club that locals seemed to both respect and fear. The kind of guys who could probably snap bones without breaking a sweat. But the way they looked at their women wasn't just gentle.

It was pure love. And they didn't care who knew.

I couldn't help but think about the way Wesley had cuddled me this morning, holding me as though I belonged in his arms. And of how he hadn't hesitated to protect me—even before we really knew each other.

Then there was the way his voice went rough when he called me sunshine. And good girl.

I curled my arms a little tighter around Porter and looked back at the man I was quickly falling for. He was still watching me, his jaw tight, like he was holding back everything he wanted to say.

My heart squeezed.

I didn't know what any of this meant yet. If the way he touched me was just heat or something more. I hoped he was like his club brothers—loving, loyal, and all in with me.

10

HUNTER

Holy fucking shit.

I couldn't tear my eyes away from the sight of Sadie cradling the little baby in her arms.

She was all soft curves and sweet smiles, cooing down at the little boy. My heart squeezed, and my groin tightened. All I could think about was how soon she'd be holding our baby. The one I was going to fuck into her as soon as possible.

She was already living with me, though she hadn't realized it was permanent yet. Her cut was being made. And I'd ordered the ring last night while she slept. All that was left was to breed her. Tie her to me in every way that mattered—with unbreakable bonds.

Then her stomach growled. Sadie blushed and

kept her eyes on the baby. "Um, sorry. We forgot dinner last night. I guess I'm a little hungry."

That was on me. I should've made sure she'd eaten. I wanted to kick my own ass for not seeing to all her needs.

"You need breakfast, sunshine," I growled.

"It can wait until Ellery is done."

Whiskey took one look at my face and practically lunged across the room. "Thanks. But you should get some food." He carefully lifted Porter from her arms, nodding toward the spread at the bar. "You want him back after, you're more than welcome."

Sadie lit up, and her voice was pure sunshine. "I'm happy to help with the kids anytime."

Yeah, well, she was about to have her hands full making her own.

I curled my fingers around hers and led her to the cooking area where a massive spread covered the bar.

"Pancakes?" I asked, already grabbing a plate.

"Sure. Oh—and one of those cinnamon rolls? They look amazing."

I set one next to her pancakes. "Stone's old lady, Britta, bakes them. Damn good, but they don't hold a candle to yours."

Sadie giggled. "Those are Marcy's. You've never had my cinnamon rolls."

I leveled her with a look. "You sure about that?" My voice dropped. "Pretty sure I'm addicted to your cinnamon taste, sunshine."

Her cheeks flushed a deep pink, and she gave me a shy little smile. "I don't know. Maybe you should try it again. Just to see if your theory is correct."

My cock throbbed. I was two seconds from forgetting breakfast altogether and bending her over the damn counter. But she needed to eat, and it was my job to make sure she did.

After piling more food on her plate, I walked her to the table and set it down in front of her.

"Eat," I ordered, my voice low and rough.

She glanced up, and when she caught the heat in my eyes, she blushed all over again. "You're not hungry?"

I leaned down, brushing my lips against her ear. "Starving, sunshine. But not for food."

Her breath hitched, and my restraint fought the bands of my control.

The second her plate was clean, I stood, scooped her up, and tossed her over my shoulder. Her surprised squeal made every cell in my body light up.

I didn't say a damn word on the way back to my room. I was too focused. Too far gone.

I carried her to the bed and dropped her onto the edge of the mattress. She let out a breathless giggle, and the sound was so fucking sweet it made my chest ache.

"I can't tell you how many times I've pictured you here," I rasped, letting my fingers trail under her shirt. "In this bed. Our bed."

She laughed softly. "I'm kind of surprised how easily I slept with you wrapped around me all night. I've had a little bit of claustrophobia ever since I was six and got caught in a kiddie ride at the carnival. It was in a tunnel and so dark that I felt as though I was in there forever, even though my parents told me afterward that it only took about five minutes to rescue me."

I stroked my thumb across her cheek. "I'm so fucking sorry that happened to you, sunshine."

"It was a long time ago, and being with you seems to be helping more than anything else ever has." Unwavering trust shone from her blue orbs. "You make me feel so safe."

"Thank fuck because I'm not letting you go." I yanked the shirt over her head and tossed it aside. "You're better than every filthy dream I've ever had."

She sucked in a breath, her chest rising fast, tits straining against the thin lace of her bra. My gaze locked on the soft swells, and I watched them jiggle with each breath she dragged in. Her sky-blue eyes—bright and flushed with heat—stared up at me like I was the only man in the world.

My hand slid to her stomach, palm flattening against the soft skin. "I knew I wanted you to have my kids. But then I saw you holding that baby—and now all I can think about is flipping you onto this mattress and fucking you full until you're round with mine."

My eyes drifted up to meet her sky-blue pools, and satisfaction roared through me when I saw anticipation swirling with hot desire.

I slipped my hands to her waistband and tugged her pants and panties down in one smooth motion until she was bared to me. Then I ran my palms back up her thighs, spreading her open wide.

"Lie back," I murmured, voice low and rough as I reached up to unhook her bra. "Let me see you."

She did as she was told, and when the bra came off, her perfect tits bounced free.

"You were made for me, sunshine." I slid my thumb across a stiff peak, my dick throbbing when she shuddered. "Made to take me. To be bred by me.

And once I put my baby in you, sunshine...you won't just feel mine—you'll look it, too."

She moaned, and my dick strained against the zipper of my jeans, threatening to bust it open.

"You like the sound of that, don't you, Sadie?" I grunted as I firmly squeezed the mounds filling my hands. "Want me to fill you with my fat cock and fuck my baby into you?"

She bit her lip, and I frowned as I tugged it from between her teeth.

"Mine," I snapped. I hated it when she chewed that lip, wanting only my teeth to be the ones nibbling on it. But until now, I'd held back my level of obsession with her body.

Seeing her holding Porter, though, had the overly possessive motherfucker inside me rising to the surface, and I didn't have the strength to hold back anymore. "Everything about you is mine, sunshine. This luscious mouth—made for taking my cock down your throat. These mouthwatering tits begging to be sucked." My hands traveled to her soft, flat stomach. "This unprotected womb I'm gonna stuff full of come." I continued, caressing every part of her body as I claimed possession of it all. "And this," I growled when I reached her center and cupped it, "this young, innocent pussy is mine. I own it, do you understand, sunshine? No one but me will ever touch it. Lick it. Fucking devour it. Not even you. It's mine."

Sadie's heated skin was damp, and a pink blush spread down her body all the way to her sex. She'd never looked so damn beautiful. Her nipples were diamond hard, and her pussy drenched my hand. I pressed the heel of my hand against her little bundle of nerves, and she cried out, bucking her hips in search of more. "So damn responsive," I gritted out through clenched teeth. Gingerly, I pushed one finger into her channel, testing to see if she was still sore. A small burst of come left my cock when she moaned and clenched around the digit.

"Tell me who you belong to, sunshine," I demanded.

"You, Wesley. You own all of me."

The words were like gasoline on the fire raging inside me, and I crushed my mouth over hers, pouring all of my love and naked desire into the kiss.

My heart pounded when I ripped my lips away and pressed my forehead against hers, trying to catch my breath. When I was more in control, I pressed my fists into the mattress on both sides of her, hovering above and sweeping my gaze over her beautiful body. "Fucking gorgeous," I grunted as I trailed the pad of one finger down the valley between her tits, then paused to draw a circle around her belly button before continuing down to the naked, glistening folds of her pussy.

"Love this," I told her, my tone low and dark.

Sadie shuddered and let out a sexy little moan.

She was so much smaller than me. It was a wonder I fit inside her. But doubt had never entered my mind because I was convinced that Sadie was my perfect match. And I'd been right.

There would still be a bite of pain when I entered her, but it would mix with her pleasure to create something intoxicating.

Suddenly ravenous, I jumped to my feet and shrugged off my cut, while toeing off my boots. Then I grabbed the back of my shirt and pulled it off over my head.

Sadie's eyes roamed my chest, and she licked her lips, sending all of the blood in my body rushing south to my groin. When my hands moved to my belt, I heard a little catch in her breath and smirked.

"The way you look at me." I shook my head as I unbuckled my belt and lowered the zipper on my pants. "It makes me so fucking hot." I shoved them down, freeing my cock since I'd gone commando.

She leaned up on her elbows, and her blue orbs

were glued to my groin as I pulled my jeans off the rest of the way, wincing when my painfully hard dick slapped against my chiseled stomach.

Sadie gulped. "I saw it this morning, so why am I still shocked that it's so big?"

"Relax, sunshine," I chuckled.

She gave me a dry look and muttered, "Seriously, Wesley. You're hung like a horse."

I tossed my head back and laughed harder than I had in...I didn't know how long. I wasn't sure how I could be so fucking turned on and amused all at once. But Sadie constantly amazed me.

A devilish smile split my face as I moved to stand between her open legs.

"Talk like that isn't gonna make it any smaller," I teased.

Sadie rolled her eyes and flopped back down on the mattress with a long-suffering sigh. "Better get on with it then."

Grinning, I muttered, "Guess you're just gonna have to put up with orgasms from my fat cock for the rest of your life."

She raised her head and tried to look put out but failed when a giggle slipped out. "I'll need another example before I can really decide."

"Better get to work convincing you." I dropped to

my knees and leaned in, inhaling deeply to take her sweet scent into my lungs. "My turn for breakfast."

Sadie moaned, and her hands twisted in the bedspread as she raised her hips up like an offering.

"Such a good girl," I grunted before I buried my face between her thighs.

I ate her juicy pussy like a man getting his first meal after years of fasting.

"Wesley," she whined, her hands delving into my hair so she could hold my head to her core. Her low, throaty voice and the sting from her grip on my hair sent fire racing through my veins. By the time I'd had my fill, she'd come twice, screaming my name.

I stood and helped her move up to the center of the bed, then crawled over her.

When my body covered hers, sparks ignited everywhere we touched. My cock jerked and spurted come when I rocked it into her hot center.

"Fuck. So damn hot." When I moved again, her folds split and her arousal coated my dick. "So fucking wet. Damn, I need to be inside you."

"Wesley, please," Sadie whimpered, thrusting her pelvis up and digging her nails into my shoulders.

"Shit," I grunted when I felt the sting all the way in my core. "Gonna make me lose control and shove my cock into your little pussy like a battering ram again, sunshine."

"Yes," she begged. "I need you, Wesley."

She didn't have to ask me twice. I opened her legs a little wider to make more room for me, then changed my position so the swollen head of my shaft kissed her opening. Her tits jiggled from her heavy breathing, and I bent my head, sucking on one of her rosy nipples.

Sadie moaned, and her body writhed, desperate with need.

Unlike the first time when I'd popped her cherry with one thrust, I entered her slowly. Savoring the way it felt to slide through her wetness and push into the tight grip of her inner walls. Then I released her nipple with a pop, blowing on the glistening bud. I gave the other breast the same treatment, and when I couldn't hold back any longer, I punched my hips forward, sheathing me completely.

"Wesley!" she cried, her nails digging into my shoulders again.

"Holy fucking hell."

Her channel was still virgin tight, and the grip it had on my cock was almost painful, spiking my pleasure. Black spots danced in front of my eyes, and I blinked a few times, trying to clear my head and regain some control.

Sadie made a muffled noise, and my gaze shot to her face.

"Don't," I growled.

"W-what?" she asked dazedly.

"I want to hear you, sunshine. Every moan, every whimper, every scream. Who do those belong to, Sadie?" I punctuated the question with a hard thrust.

"Ah!" she cried out, bucking her hips.

"Who?" I grunted.

"You, Wesley. You."

"Look at me, Sadie," I ordered.

Slowly, her eyelids lifted, and my body clenched. My dick spurted a blast of jizz as she stared up at me with dark blue orbs, filled to the brim with need and passion.

"Damn straight."

My cock flexed, and she moaned. "I need more, Wesley. Please!"

Her inner walls throbbed, milking my cock, taking me closer to my climax.

I wasn't ready to come, so I took several deep breaths and found my center, just like when I was about to pull the trigger on my sniper rifle. When I felt a little more in control, I pulled out and slowly pushed back in.

"More," she begged.

"Such a greedy girl," I grunted. "Hungry for my cock, baby?"

She nodded frantically.

Shifting up onto my knees, I draped her legs over my arms so her pelvis was raised and my cock would hit all the right places every time I drove inside. Staring down at our connection, I was fascinated as I watched my shaft disappear inside her, then reappear covered in her cream. "Fuck. It's so damn hot, seeing you take me like such a good girl. Watching my cock claim you over and over."

She shuddered with pleasure, her muscles rippling around my steel rod. The sensation was too much, and without thinking, I punched my hips forward, slamming into her.

"Shit!" I cursed, immediately stilling. "Alright?"

"Don't stop, Wesley," Sadie moaned. "You feel so good."

"Don't know if I can hold back," I panted.

Sadie's hands slid down to her pussy, and she spread the lips apart. She was soaked, her juices dripping down her thighs, and her pink clit was hard and swollen, popping out of its hood. So fucking needy.

"I need you, Wesley. Make me come. Fill me up. I want it all."

I fucking broke.

My animal instincts took over, and I pounded in and out of her pussy, driving as deep as possible every time. I was gonna do exactly what she asked. Stuff her so full of my come there would be no fucking way she wasn't knocked up.

"Yes!" she hissed, her body clenching hard with pleasure every time I bottomed out, the tip of my dick ramming against her cervix.

"Take it all, sunshine," I growled. "Fuck, that's it. Suck my cock deep inside you. Yes! Fuck!"

I'd learned really fast that the filthier my words were, the harder she climaxed and the more of my seed she'd suck up inside her.

"Oh yes! Wesley! Yes! Yes!" She shoved her hands in her hair, grasping the strands as she writhed and bucked, trembling on the edge of her orgasm.

I fucked her like a damn animal intent on claiming and breeding its mate. The bed hit the wall with the force of my thrusts, and the mattress springs squeaked in protest.

"Oh fuck, Sadie! Spread those thighs even more for me—fuck!"

She widened her legs until there was a wince of pain on her face.

"Good girl," I gritted out through a clenched jaw. Then I pushed them back toward her chest and dug my knees into the bed. Sweat dripped down my chest as I fucked her with nothing but pure instinct. I had no control over my mind or body.

"Oh fuck, Sadie! Fuck! Oh fuck, yes!"

Her body shuddered violently, then a scream ripped straight from her soul as she shattered beneath me.

Like a rogue wave, my climax crashed into me, tossing me every which way until I didn't know up from down. My cock exploded, shooting jets of hot come inside her, stuffing her full just like I'd promised.

"Whoa," Sadie wheezed.

"Yeah," I agreed, breathing hard as I collapsed on top of her.

Mindful of my weight, I rolled to my back, keeping my shaft planted inside her.

"How...?" Sadie blinked when she wiggled and realized I was still hard.

I shrugged. "Told you. I'm addicted."

She giggled and rested her chin on my chest,

gazing up at me with a cheeky grin. "Or maybe it's not convinced its job is done yet."

I raised a brow and rocked into her, making her moan. "You trying to get fucked again, sunshine?"

"Um...no," she lied, her face turning red as she glanced away.

I cupped her chin and guided her head back so she was looking into my eyes. "Don't ever be embarrassed to ask for what you want, sunshine. Especially not in bed."

"Okay," she whispered, her sweet smile returning.

"Now, answer my question. Looking to get fucked again, baby?"

"Yes."

"Good girl."

11

SADIE

If someone had told me a week ago that I'd be showing up to work with a six-foot-something, leather-wearing biker shadowing my every move, I probably would've laughed. But I couldn't be happier about it.

Wesley held the door to the bakery open for me, his hand settling on the small of my back as I stepped inside. I couldn't help teasing him as we walked through the front of the shop. "You know, this might be a record for the grumpiest bodyguard in bakery history."

A grunt came from behind me. "Not your bodyguard."

"No?" I glanced at him over my shoulder.

"Because you've been doing a pretty good impression."

"Being mine comes with perks."

"Perks, huh?" I turned to grin up at him. "Like the kind you gave me last night...and again this morning even though we had to be up super early?"

His eyes dropped to my mouth. "Plenty more where those came from, sunshine."

My knees nearly buckled on the spot, but I managed to play it off by grabbing an apron off the hook. Wesley settled onto one of the stools near the prep counter, crossing his arms and scanning the room like he expected an ambush to come out of the muffin trays.

Marcy walked in from her office with her usual bouncy energy and came to a full stop.

Her eyes flicked to Wesley. Then to me. Then back to Wesley.

"Well," she said, drawing out the word. "I'm not one to brag when I'm right, but...."

I straightened quickly as she trailed off. "Good morning!"

"Good morning, indeed." Her eyes sparkled as she moved past Wesley, who gave her a silent nod of acknowledgment. "Is this the part where I pretend not to notice the glowering biker watching your every move like a lion guarding a cupcake?"

I choked on a laugh. "He's just...umm...making sure everything's safe."

"Uh-huh." She arched a brow. "Is that what the kids are calling it these days?"

I ducked my head and tried to focus on frosting a batch of cupcakes, my face burning.

"Back in a second," Wesley murmured before striding out of the kitchen.

"So..." Marcy drawled, voice low and knowing. "You gonna tell me what it's like to have an Iron Rogue look at you like he's two seconds away from carrying you off over his shoulder, or do I have to keep guessing?"

My eyes widened. "What? No, it's not...he was just being—"

Marcy laughed, holding up a hand. "Relax, I'm not judging. Just making an observation. A very accurate one."

I bit my lip and looked down, my cheeks growing hotter.

"Oh my god," Marcy breathed. "You like it."

I let out a small, helpless laugh. "I don't know! He's just so...intense."

"Uh-huh." Marcy smirked. "That man came in

here with a predator stare, installed four cameras when I only approved one, and looked like he was one wrong answer away from ripping Austin in half the other day."

"I know," I sighed. "There must be something wrong with me because it all makes me weak in the knees."

She grinned at me. "If you pass out, I'll catch you. But if he catches you first, I'm not interfering. Hunter has clearly claimed someone in that sexy head of his."

My brows drew together. "Claimed?"

Marcy gestured toward the door with a nod. "That man is not thinking casual thoughts about you, honey. That's Iron Rogue-level interest. Which means it's not going anywhere anytime soon."

My mouth opened, then closed again since I had no clue how to respond.

"You're doomed. But like...in a good way." Marcy grabbed her apron. "Tell your cupcake lion that we've got a fresh pot of coffee brewing when he comes back, which I'm sure will be any second now. Might as well caffeinate the muscle."

"He's not—" I started, then sighed. "Okay, fine. He is."

"Damn right I am," Wesley muttered under his

breath as he walked back into the kitchen and sat down on a stool only a few feet away from me.

Marcy chuckled and headed into the walk-in fridge, and I let out a long breath. Wesley might've been quiet, but his presence was loud. Especially with how he took every bit of our surroundings in even though it was just us and Marcy in the bakery until we opened.

I wouldn't complain if he wanted to watch over me like some overprotective, brooding biker shadow.

I was halfway through smoothing the butter-cream on the last tray of cupcakes when I heard a thunk behind me. The sound wasn't loud, but it made me freeze mid-frost.

"Did something just—" I turned toward the noise and saw the prep table wobbling slightly to one side. One of the legs had slipped, the bolt connecting it clearly working its way loose. "Oh no."

Marcy peeked out of the walk-in with a raised brow. "Something else broke?"

I sighed. "Yeah. I'll text Austin to swing by later and—"

"No," Wesley cut in, sharp and immediate.

Both Marcy and I looked at him. He was already on his feet, moving toward the table with a quiet intensity that made my breath catch. He knelt to inspect the loose bolt, then glanced up at me.

"You're not calling anyone." His voice was low and final. "I'll fix it."

I blinked. "Do you know how?"

He gave me a look that told me how foolish my question was. Then he pulled a multitool from his back pocket like he'd been waiting for an excuse to use it. "I can handle a loose bolt."

Marcy ducked back into the walk-in, smirking to herself, and I bit my lip.

"Well, I mean...if you're going to start fixing things around here," I murmured, trying to sound casual even as I felt my cheeks heating again, "I should probably get you a tool belt. You can wear it without a shirt."

Wesley's head tilted, and the corner of his mouth twitched.

I held up my hands quickly. "Actually, no. Scratch that. Too many people come through this bakery, and no one needs to see that but me."

His eyes darkened as he straightened to his full height, the multitool clicking shut in his palm. "That right?"

I nodded fast, trying not to squirm under the heat in his gaze. "Definitely."

He stepped closer and murmured, "You want me shirtless in a tool belt, you'll get it. But only for you, sunshine."

I could've melted into a puddle on the floor right then and there. Instead, I managed to squeak, "Good. Great. Love that plan."

His smirk went full-blown as he stepped around me, brushing a kiss to the top of my head as though he hadn't just made my panties spontaneously combust.

I was still trying to cool off from the mental image of Wesley in nothing but jeans and a tool belt when my phone buzzed in the pocket of my apron. I pulled it out and smiled at the screen.

"It's my parents," I told him.

His brows lifted just slightly. "You gonna answer?"

I hesitated for a second, suddenly shy. "They're video calling. If I'm not driving, they like to see my face when they talk since they're going to be gone for so long."

"Can't fault them for that. Go ahead and answer."

I tapped to accept, and my parents' faces filled the screen—Dad in a ball cap and hoodie, Mom with windblown hair and a huge smile.

"There she is!" Mom beamed. "Hi, honey!"

"Hey," I said, suddenly feeling sixteen again instead of nineteen.

"Sorry to bother you at work, but at least we caught you before the bakery opens." Her eyes narrowed as she leaned toward the camera. "Wait a second...why do you look like you've just been necking with someone?"

"Mom!"

"Just saying," she laughed. "You've got that look that I've seen on my own face after your dad has given me a big smooch."

I shook my head. "Did you really have to go there?"

Dad's gaze darted over my shoulder, and he cleared his throat pointedly. "Who are you?"

"Hunter," Wesley replied before I could answer.

I startled slightly but didn't pull the phone away as he moved to stand next to me.

My mom blinked. "Oh, my. You're very...tall."

Wesley's mouth twitched. "Yes, ma'am."

Dad gave a slow nod, his voice calm but firm. "So how exactly do you know our daughter?"

Wesley didn't miss a beat. "I met her a few days ago. She started working at the bakery in our territory. Someone left her a threatening note. I handled it."

"You handled it," Dad repeated, not quite a question.

"Yes, sir."

There was a long pause before Dad finally said, "And are you planning to keep handling it?"

Wesley's gaze didn't waver. "I don't plan to leave her side."

Dad studied him for another second, then gave a slow nod. "Alright. I appreciate you looking out for her."

"Always will," Wesley said quietly.

My eyes widened when my dad's attention switched back to me. "I'd ask why this is the first I'm hearing about the note, but I'm pretty damn sure the answer won't make me much happier."

I gulped. "Um..."

"Well." Mom clapped her hands, saving me from needing to respond. "Sounds like we won't need to cut the RV trip short since Hunter has things well in hand."

"Unless we need to meet him in person," Dad muttered.

"Maybe once you're back on this side of the

country," I said quickly, cheeks blazing. "And I'll make chess pie."

That earned a smile from both of them.

"Be good, sweetie," Mom said. "And call again tomorrow."

"Love you," I whispered.

"Love you too," they said in unison before the call ended.

I lowered the phone slowly, heaving a relieved sigh over how well that went, considering.

Wesley didn't say anything. He just reached out and brushed his knuckles down my cheek.

Somehow, introducing him to my parents made everything feel more real.

12

HUNTER

Sadie leaned into my touch, and I curled an arm around her waist, pulling her against my body. My lips brushed her forehead, and she sighed, melting into me.

The call with her parents had gone pretty well, in my estimation. Knowing I was there to keep his little girl safe from real danger had gone a long way in smoothing things over with her dad. Hopefully, he wouldn't get overprotective when it was all over and try to chase me away. It was never gonna happen, and the faster he came to terms with it, the less strain it would put on Sadie. Besides, I was pretty sure he'd come around when he saw how much Sadie meant to me. How much I loved and worshipped her and would do anything for her.

"My mom will support our relationship," Sadie mused as she rubbed her nose on my chest. "My dad won't be as easy, but I have no doubt you'll charm him."

I heard a snorted laugh behind me and turned to see Maverick standing a few feet away. His feet were braced apart, and his arms were folded across his chest, emphasizing his muscular build. Most people would be intimidated, but even if I'd felt a little of that, it was ruined by the amused twist of his lips and laughing eyes.

Apparently, Marcy had opened for business while we were chatting with Sadie's parents.

"Charm, huh?" Maverick drawled. "Not exactly Hunter's strong suit. Guy's more steel wool than smooth talk."

"You're confusing charm with not giving a fuck what people think," I grunted.

Maverick snorted. "Guess that explains why your idea of flirting is glaring and grunting in her general direction."

"Worked on Sadie, didn't it?" I shot back, tightening my arm around her waist.

Sadie let out a soft, breathy laugh, her cheeks pink as she peeked up at me with a smile that made my chest feel too tight.

"I think I liked that you didn't try to charm me."

Maverick chuckled, rubbing a hand over his jaw as he shook his head.

"Shit, the universe really outdid itself sending you someone that sweet," he said, smirking. "She's gotta be custom-built, man. 'Cause no one else on earth would be charmed by a grumpy-as-shit motherfucker like you."

Sadie giggled and ducked her head as she turned to head back behind the counter.

I watched her go, my gaze glued to the soft sway of her hips.

Then my eyes traveled up, and my gut clenched when I thought about her wearing my vest. I couldn't wait to see my name stitched across her back like a warning.

All anyone else saw was the sweet sunshine. Innocence wrapped in sugar and cinnamon.

Only I knew better.

I knew what she sounded like when she moaned my name in the dark.

How she looked with her lips swollen, and her thighs trembling.

And how tight her pussy gripped my cock when she came apart beneath me, her body knowing exactly who it belonged to.

She wasn't just soft.

She was mine.

And I'd burn the whole fucking town to the ground if anyone tried to take her from me.

She disappeared through the door to the kitchen with one last glance over her shoulder, her blue pools dancing with happiness and my chest clenched like I'd taken a hit point-blank.

I wanted to put that look on her face every day for the rest of our lives. Even when she wore my ring, my vest, my name, and carried my kid, it would never be enough. I'd prove to her every day that she belonged to me and do everything in my power to make her happy.

Forever wasn't a concept. It was a promise. And even though she hadn't known it, she'd agreed to exactly that the first time she smiled at me.

Mav clapped me on the back in that gruff way of his that meant he gave a shit, then went to the counter and ordered from Marcy.

I gave him a chin lift before heading back to the kitchen to tighten the loose bolt since I'd gotten distracted earlier. When I finished, I popped a quick kiss on Sadie's luscious mouth, then returned to the front of the shop.

My stomach growled, so I looked over the pastries, trying to decide what to eat.

Sadie bounced back out of the kitchen with a tray of cinnamon rolls, and when her eyes met mine, my lips curled up into a wicked grin.

Her cheeks turned pink while her sky-blue orbs darkened to sapphire.

"Gonna need one of your cinnamon rolls, sunshine," I murmured.

Her breath hitched, making my smile grow. She shook it off after a foggy second and shot me an admonishing frown. "Behave."

My eyebrows shot up to my hairline before I burst into laughter. When my mirth died down, I noticed Sadie, Marcy, and the two other customers in the bakery staring at me like I'd grown two heads.

Their shock was understandable. Before Sadie, my personality was permanently locked in "grumpy-as-shit motherfucker" mode, as Mav had said. Only my own personal sunshine dragged me into the light.

Sadie beamed at me as she put a roll on a plate and fixed me a black coffee.

"Let me know if these are as good as mine," she said with a saucy wink.

I leaned in so no one could hear my deep, gritty

voice except her. "Nothing in the world tastes as sweet as your pussy, sunshine."

Sadie blushed tomato-red, making me smirk as I took my breakfast and went to find a seat. I chose a table off to the side, with a clear view of the entire bakery. While I stayed alert for anything suspicious happening around me, I set out the laptop I'd brought to get some work done.

Although I had a healthy bank account from saving during my years in the military and FBI, my investments had also paid off. Plus, I got a cut from certain MC income streams, so I wouldn't ever be hurting for money. However, I still considered opportunities that came my way—usually consulting or teaching.

My eyes tracked Sadie for a few minutes before I focused on my email and saw a message from someone I'd met while teaching a few seminars at Quantico. He owned a security firm and hoped I'd teach a series of workshops at a retreat for his employees.

I wasn't opposed to the idea, but when I saw the location for the event, I grinned.

Maui.

Thoughts of a hut on a private beach with my woman in a skimpy bikini—or better yet, naked—

filled my head. I shot a reply to my friend, telling him
I'd check my schedule but was definitely interested.

I managed to finish a few more tasks while
watching Sadie. She fascinated me; even just the
simple act of maneuvering around the shop kept my
attention glued on her. Her movements were fluid
and unintentionally sensual, and whenever she
smiled at someone, my chest burned with jealousy. It
wasn't rational, but nor would it ever change, so I
didn't bother trying.

After we'd been there a couple of hours, my gut
suddenly tightened when the bell over the door
jingled. Glancing up, I scowled when I saw that little
punk Austin saunter into the place with a cocky
smile that said he thought he was God's gift to
women.

He must have felt my eyes on him because his
head turned, and when he spotted me, his smile
slipped and his steps faltered. But then he straightened his shoulders and turned away, once again
headed to the counter.

Our gazes hadn't clashed for long, but it was
enough for me to see a spark of anger. And something a little darker. The kid set off all kinds of alarm
bells inside me, but right then, I had no tangible
reason. Still, I monitored him closely, especially

when he came to a stop in front of Sadie and greeted her with a cocky smirk.

"Good morning, Sadie."

His voice was higher than it should be for a twenty-year-old guy, and it grated on my nerves.

"Um, hey, Austin," Sadie replied, her gaze darting nervously over to me before returning to him.

"You know what I like," he murmured, his tone suggestive.

Sadie's cheeks heated, but not from desire. Her feet shuffled uncomfortably, and her sky-blue orbs darkened with annoyance.

I moved my chair back, but I didn't get up yet, waiting to see where the interaction went before possibly causing a scene.

"Sure. Almond latte and blueberry scone."

What kind of man ate shit like that?

"I'm glad you haven't had anything else breaking around here. But if you're ever worried about it, let me know, and I'll take a look. Maybe fix it before it breaks."

Time to put this fucker in his place.

I pushed to my feet and started toward them while Sadie went to the espresso machine to work on his order.

"Actually," she said conversationally, "the prep table was wonky this morning, but Wesley fixed it."

Austin's whole body tensed, and he shot a look my way that had those alarm bells blaring like a fire truck.

He tried to hide his anger and resentment but did a piss-poor job of it.

My eyes narrowed in warning, and he huffed, turning back to Sadie and practically snatching his food from her before stomping out the door. His lack of attention almost sent him barreling straight into Midnight and Phoenix.

I nodded at my brothers, and while Phoenix continued to peruse the glass cases of food, Midnight made a beeline for me.

"Got news," he muttered as he dropped onto the chair opposite me.

I was surprised to hear that because he'd called me the day after Sadie received the note and told me there'd been no prints on it, leaving us with a dead end in that direction.

"Deviant find something?" It was unlikely that he would have told Midnight before me, but it was the only explanation for his news that I could think of.

"Yeah, but I only know because I gave him the lead."

I waited impatiently for him to elaborate, tapping my fingers on the table.

"Thinking back on the situation after I didn't find anything on the note, it occurred to me that it got into the mailbox somehow. They'd been meticulous with the paper, but had they been as careful with the metal box? So I came by yesterday and dusted it. Got five hits."

I thought over the options and murmured, "The mailman, Marcy, Sadie, and me. Who was the fifth?"

"Austin Collins. He's Geoff's son. The owner of—"

"The hardware store," I interrupted through clenched teeth. "I know."

"Right. Told Deviant, and he dived into the kid."

"He find any shit that hints at Austin having a history?"

Midnight shook his head, leaning back in his chair and crossing his arms. "Didn't come across anything official. Even when he went deeper, there didn't seem to be any kind of pattern."

"Could just mean this is the first time he's gone off the deep end for a woman."

I knew something had been off with that little bastard.

"Could be," Midnight agreed. "If so, behavior like that shouldn't go unchecked. Next time could be worse, and someone might get hurt."

My hands clenched into fists and fury built inside me. "Sounds like the motherfucker needs a visit to The Room."

"The Room" was a small building on Iron Rogues' property built on a spot that was the farthest from any of the businesses, homes, and clubhouse. From the outside, it looked a lot like the safehouses we had throughout the south. We used the moniker because it was as dismissive as its exterior. But on the inside, it was very different. The interior had four rooms, a lounging area of sorts, a cell, an interrogation hold, an armory, and a storage space that had a cache of *tools* that might be needed to aid us in gaining what we wanted.

"Need you to send a couple of prospects here to watch over Sadie," I growled as I packed up my shit.

He agreed and went outside to make the call.

I quickly pulled my woman aside. "Gotta go handle some club business, sunshine. But you'll have a couple of rooks here to protect you."

Sadie clasped her hands together and worried her bottom lip.

I was concerned that she might push for more information. We hadn't really had the talk about her role in the club as an old lady and that she'd have to accept that there would always be things I couldn't share with her.

But she shocked the shit out of me again.

"You can't tell me anything, right?"

"Yeah. I won't ever lie to you, sunshine. Or keep things from you. Unless it's club business. Can you handle that?"

"Of course." Her answer was immediate, and I was tempted to drag her to the back and fuck her because she was so damn amazing. "Is it dangerous?"

"Not for me," I said honestly. "Since this involves you, I can at least say you won't need to worry about getting more notes or broken windows again. Turns out Austin was behind it, and I'm gonna make sure he knows to stay the fuck away from you from now on."

"Wow, I never would've guessed." Her nose scrunched. "Do you think that's why we had so many things break around here even though Marcy bought all new equipment? Because he wanted to see me?"

"It's a safe bet, sunshine," I confirmed with a nod.

"Ugh, what a jerk," she muttered. "I know it's just Austin, but...be careful anyway."

"Always, sunshine."

I gave her a deep, soul-stealing kiss before focusing on what came next.

My shoulders were tight with tension when I walked into the interrogation hold where Austin was cuffed to a small metal chair.

It hadn't taken long to find him because the asshole had been lingering near the bakery, out of sight, but with a clear view of the building.

"Shoulda moved the fuck on the first time you realized Sadie was under Iron Rogue protection," I grunted. "When it was clear she was mine, you shoulda forgotten she even existed."

"Fucking Rogues," he spat. "I could have had her if you bastards hadn't been around constantly."

My knuckles cracked when I clenched my hands into fists and sauntered closer until I was right in front of him. "Bullshit. She was always gonna be mine. You were just too cocky and stupid to see it."

"What-the fuck-ever," he snarked. He was trying to be brave, but I could see the fear in his eyes.

A sinister smile crawled across my face. "Should check that attitude, asshole. Or the lesson you're about to get will be much worse."

"Hunter."

I exhaled harshly and spun around, frustrated as hell. The prez wouldn't have come here himself if he wasn't gonna tell me something that would piss me the fuck off.

"It can't go this way. He's a fucking local. He disappears, we'll have the law on our ass, and it won't matter how many we own. They won't have a choice."

"Fuck!" I shouted, punching my fist down into the metal table set out to hold any supplies we brought in for interrogation purposes.

"Had a talk with his dad. Seems the kid has already been fucking up in other ways, and this was the last straw."

Austin snorted. "Like he can do anything to me. I'm an adult."

"You're a twisted fuck," Fox spat at him, then looked at me again. "Geoff's got shit on him that will force his cooperation when he sends him away."

"And if he fixates on another woman?" I seethed.

"We'll have eyes on him all the time. Anywhere he goes. Geoff knows that if the little shit screws up again, we'll be handling it our way."

I hated the plan. It filled me with murderous rage. But I'd pledged to follow Fox's orders. And truthfully, he was the prez for a reason.

He would never get in the way of a brother's lust for revenge or punishment to anyone who deserved it unless he had to. In this case, I knew he was right. No matter how much I wanted to shout and rage that he was wrong.

I closed my eyes and dropped my head back, breathing deeply. After a few minutes, my heart rate slowed and I nodded at Fox, letting him know I had my shit under control.

Then he grinned. "Doesn't mean he'll leave here without learning somethin'."

I should've known he'd have my back in any way he could.

Turning around, I prowled over to stand in front of Austin, and the evil smirk reappeared on my face.

"Always been a damn good instructor," I grunted right before my boot slammed down on his balls.

13

SADIE

I was trying so hard to stay calm, but my nerves were fraying by the second. I sat curled on the worn leather couch in the clubhouse common room, pretending to sip the coffee I didn't really want. I was a nervous wreck, which was why Marcy told me to head out only five minutes after Wesley left the bakery for whatever his club business was.

"They'll be back soon," Ellery said gently from the chair across from me. She bounced Porter on her knee, giving me a warm, reassuring smile. "And you know that guy is no match for Hunter."

"Not sure much of anyone is," Marnie added from the other end of the couch.

I let out a shaky laugh. "Yeah. I know you're right. It's just hard to sit here and wait."

Dahlia, the prez's wife, nodded. "Girl, I get it. The waiting is the worst part when shit is going down, big or small."

I gave them a watery smile, grateful they weren't trying to tell me to calm down. Just be with me.

"I didn't think I'd be like this," I admitted quietly. "It's only been a few days, and I already—" I broke off, unsure how to finish that sentence without sounding completely unhinged.

But Ellery did it for me. "You already love him."

My cheeks heated, but I didn't deny it. Because it was true.

I didn't confirm it either. I wanted the first time I said it to be to Wesley.

The distant rumble of engines cut through the air—and my heart stopped in my chest.

I knew Wesley would be fine since there was no chance Austin could successfully take him on, especially with his club brothers at his back. But every sound made my heart stutter while I waited.

Finally, the rumble of engines grew close. Loud, deep, and familiar to me now.

I shot to my feet before the bikes had even fully rolled into the lot, my heart slamming against my ribs. Racing out of the clubhouse, I was out the door before his boot hit the pavement.

He looked up at the sound of my footsteps, and the second our eyes locked, the rest of the world fell away.

"Sad—"

He didn't even get my whole name out before I threw myself at him. His arms wrapped around me instantly, catching me midair as though it was the most natural thing in the world. I buried my face in his neck, breathing him in, clinging to him like I never wanted to let go.

And I didn't.

He held me just as tightly, one of his big hands curling protectively around the back of my head, the other wrapped low around my waist.

"I have you, sunshine," he murmured, voice gravelly.

I nodded against his throat, trying to keep my tears in check and failing miserably. "I know. I just— needed you to come back safe."

"Wasn't much risk of the kid doing anything to me." He leaned back slightly, just enough to tip my chin up so I'd look at him. His thumb wiped away a tear rolling down my cheek. "I'm not going anywhere, sunshine."

"You better not," I whispered.

His eyes softened. "Never."

Wesley hadn't let go of me—not completely—and I didn't want him to. I felt anchored in his arms, like everything was finally okay again. And I knew it would only stay that way as long as he was with me.

"I thought I was handling everything fine," I whispered, brushing my fingers along the edge of his cut. "But the second you were gone, I realized I wasn't okay. Not without you."

His expression turned fierce, as though I'd just confessed something sacred.

"Sadie," he said, his voice low and rough, "I love you."

I sucked in a sharp breath. My heart did this silly fluttery thing in my chest, and my eyes filled again because I felt it in every part of me—he meant those three little words. All that protectiveness and quiet intensity wasn't just about the broken window and note. It was me. It had always been me.

"I love you, too," I said, my voice barely more than a whisper. "So much."

He kissed me hard. Not rushed, not wild. Just deep and consuming, as though he needed to make sure I felt what he just said all the way to my bones.

We might've stayed wrapped up in each other forever if it hadn't been for a familiar voice behind us.

"Figured you'd be needing this," Fox called.

We broke apart, and something hit Wesley in the chest.

He caught the leather vest without breaking our eye contact, and I realized instantly what it was.

My heart stopped.

Wesley turned the leather around so I could see the patch on the back—Property of Hunter.

My breath caught. "You really want—"

"I told you I wasn't going anywhere," he said, slipping the vest over my shoulders as though he was wrapping me in armor. "This makes it official."

It was everything I'd never even let myself hope for. And he didn't stop there.

Wesley cupped my face with both hands, his thumbs sweeping along my cheeks as though he needed to feel me breathe.

"You're mine, Sadie." His tone was soft but fierce. "Not just today. Or until this shit blows over. Always."

I nodded, swallowing hard. "I want that, too."

His gaze dipped, then rose to meet mine again. His amber eyes were determined. "I want you to be my old lady."

My breath caught.

"My wife and the mother of my kids." His hands

slid down to rest on my waist, then lower. One of them flattened over my stomach. His palm was warm and steady. "Hopefully soon."

My knees nearly gave out.

"You—" I swallowed again, heart thundering. "You think I could be—?"

His deep chuckle rolled over me, sending goose bumps in its wake. "Hell yeah, you could be. I sure as fuck have done my best to make it happen in the short time I've had you in my bed."

He reached into his cut and pulled out a small black box. It was plain but perfect.

I gasped as he flicked the top open with his thumb. Inside was a delicate diamond ring, sparkling in the sunlight as though it had been waiting for this exact moment.

He plucked the ring out of the box. "I'm not waiting to make you mine."

It wasn't a question, but I still whispered, "Okay. Yes."

His eyes flared as he slowly slipped the ring on my finger. I watched it settle into place, feeling as though the beautiful diamond had always belonged there.

My fingers curled over his as I admired the ring,

heart still racing. "My parents are going to want to know right away."

He smirked. "Another reason to call them soon."

I blinked. "What do you mean?"

"If they want to see us get married, they need to start making their way back to Tennessee because I'm not waiting for our wedding. No dragging this out. You're mine, sunshine. And I want it official."

I laughed, my heart so full I thought it might burst. "Okay, then. Let's do it."

The kiss he gave me wasn't sweet—it was a promise.

And I knew my parents needed to hurry home because I'd be wearing white before the end of the week if Wesley had his way.

EPILOGUE
HUNTER

The sun was just barely peeking through the blinds when I woke up. My arms instinctively tightened around Sadie, and I tucked her even closer against me. She sighed, and when she brushed some hair out of her face, her ring caught the light.

Satisfaction and a contentment that I didn't even know existed settled in my bones.

Everything I loved in this world was lying in bed with me. And today, I was gonna bind her to me in one more way. All that would be left was putting my kid inside her. I grinned as my hand moved down to splay over her stomach. Probably had already, considering how hard I'd been working at it.

Sadie yawned and opened her eyes, the sky-blue orbs sleepy but sparkling with happiness.

"Happy wedding day," she giggled.

"'Bout fucking time," I muttered, making her laugh.

"Five days, caveman."

That was how long it took her parents to hightail it back home. "Five whole fucking days, sunshine."

She patted my chest and peered up at me through her lashes. "I'll make it up to you tonight."

In the blink of an eye, she was on her back with my body hovering over hers. "How about you make it up to me right now?"

Before she could reply, someone started pounding on my door.

"I let you talk me out of spending the night apart, Hunter," her mom yelled. "But she needs to get ready for the wedding, so hand her over!"

I cursed, wishing she was one of my brothers so I could tell them to fuck off.

"She's right," Sadie whispered with another cute giggle. "Besides, I want you to be surprised when you see me walk down the aisle."

"Fuck," I grumbled. "Fine. But this is the last time I let you go."

"I'll see you in a few hours."

My expression and tone were fierce when I replied. "And you'll belong to me. No one else."

"Hunter!" her mom yelled again.

"Be right there, Mom!" Sadie called back.

Sighing, I rolled off my soon-to-be wife and let her climb out of bed. She quickly dressed in a pair of sweats, then flitted around the room gathering her shit while I dragged on a pair of jeans. When she had everything, she started for the door, but I captured her hand and dragged her back against me, taking her mouth in a kiss that came from the depths of my soul. By the time I let her go, she was trembling and dazed, lost in a cloud of lust.

"See you at the altar, sunshine."

Sadie's mom glared at me when I finally opened the door, but I just stared back at her, completely unrepentant.

She huffed in annoyance, but her lips curled up into an amused smile as they turned away.

A couple of hours later, I was pacing in the open, grassy area behind the club where we'd decided to hold the ceremony.

"Wow," Molly chirped when she saw me. "You clean up good, Hunter."

My eyes darted around for Maverick in case he took a swing at me. Didn't matter that I wasn't the one who said it. We weren't exactly rational when it came to our women.

Relieved when I didn't spot him, I frowned at Molly. "You trying to ruin Sadie's wedding day?"

"Of course not!" Molly protested with a scowl.

"Then don't say shit that could get my face messed up before she walks down the aisle."

"I see your point," she conceded with a chuckle. "It's still true, though."

I glanced down at my dark pants and loose white shirt. It was casual by a lot of standards but definitely a step up for me. I hadn't worn a suit unless an assignment called for it since I left the FBI.

Sadie had asked me if I was going to wear something formal, but I tossed the idea out real fast.

I'd told her that she was marrying me...not a fucking tux. I followed that up by backing her into a wall and growling that she could wear nothing at all if she wanted—but the dress wouldn't last long either way.

The back door to the club opened again, banging against the wall as a woman marched outside. Her expression was fierce as she looked around, then her eyes widened as she took in the decorations, chairs, and reception setup.

"Hi," Molly greeted her with a smile. "Can I help you?"

"I'm so sorry to interrupt. I didn't realize...I just..."

"How the fuck did you even get inside the compound?" I growled.

She flinched, and Molly shot me a glare.

"I told the guy at the gate that I'm from the community center, and he called someone, then told me to wait inside. But, um, everyone who walked by ignored me...and now I see why. I didn't realize, and I got kinda mad, so I"—her hand fluttered, gesturing at the setup—"well, you know the rest."

Molly approached her and put a reassuring hand on her shoulder. "How can we help?"

"I need to talk to whoever is in charge of your money."

My eyebrows shot up. Seemed too bold for a manipulative gold digger. But who the fuck knew what went on in people's minds.

"That would be Phoenix," Molly told her. "He'll be attending the wedding in a little bit, but if it's an emergency, I'll make sure you talk to him first."

The woman nodded. "I swear, this is really important."

"Okay, follow me."

Molly started for the clubhouse, and the other

woman followed, her eyes straightforward, avoiding my piercing stare.

"Phoenix is your money guy?" she asked.

"Yep. The club treasurer. He's brilliant."

Just before they disappeared, the woman snorted in derision. "He can't be that good if he hasn't noticed someone robbing him blind."

That comment got me curious, but I didn't have time to think about anything else. I was too busy talking myself out of storming the clubhouse and dragging my woman to the altar, whether she was ready or not.

I LACED my fingers through Sadie's and guided her around the side of the clubhouse, sneaking away from the reception for a few minutes alone.

She had looked so fucking amazing when she'd stepped outside in her simple, spaghetti-strapped, white satin dress. Her hair had been floating in soft curls all around her, and her blue eyes had been bright with joy.

Fox officiated the ceremony, and despite my normal aversion to speaking around anyone but Sadie, I'd given in to her request to write our own vows. They were raw and made tears roll down her cheeks despite her beaming smile. I hadn't been able to stop myself from kissing the fuck out of her.

Just like I couldn't stop myself right now.

My mouth crashed down over hers, and she moaned, clinging to me like she didn't have the strength to stand on her own. Our tongues tangled and our breathing became labored, the kiss raging out of control.

But I wasn't gonna fuck my wife with so many people all around.

When I pulled away, Sadie leaned into my chest, her fingers playing with my patch.

"Told you I'd take care of you." I threaded my fingers through her hair. "Anything you want. It's yours."

"You've already given me everything."

I brushed my hand low on her belly and whispered, "Not everything yet."

Sadie giggled, dropping her head back to look up at me. "As hard as you've been trying, you might have."

Grinning, I lowered my lips until they were a breath away from hers. "If not, I'll just have to double down."

She gasped. "We'd never leave the bed!"

"Exactly," I murmured before I pressed my mouth to hers and gave her a slow, possessive kiss as the night wrapped around us—soft and dark, just like us.

"Mine," I growled against her lips. "You are my whole world, sunshine. I'll never let you go."

EPILOGUE
SADIE

I f someone had told me five years ago that I'd be decorating a cake while six months pregnant, covered in powdered sugar, with frosting in my hair, while my toddler sang "Wheels on the Bus" at the top of her lungs...I never would've believed them. That was how fast I fell for Wesley. And how completely he flipped my world upside down.

Not that I was complaining.

"Well, that's one way to decorate," Marcy called over the music and chaos, her voice light as she hip-checked the walk-in fridge door closed. "Pretty sure the mixer's got more icing than the cake does."

"That's not my fault." I stepped back from the counter, one hand braced on the small of my back. "Tell that to your future protégé."

Our daughter sat proudly on a step stool beside me, her curly hair half clipped up with a tiny bow and her cheeks streaked with flour. She was supposed to be holding the piping bag. Instead, she'd gotten distracted and was now smearing pink icing across the countertop like it was finger paint.

"Tell Auntie Marcy you're creating edible art," I whispered.

"Ed-a-bull aht!" she declared proudly, licking her fingers.

Marcy let out a wheeze of laughter. "Well, she's not wrong."

I reached for a clean towel and tried to wipe some of the sugar off my belly, only for the baby to give a solid kick in protest.

"Hey," I murmured, rubbing soothing circles against the bump. "You'll get your turn with the piping bag in a few years."

Or sooner, considering how strong this kid already was. My first pregnancy had been a blur of exhaustion, happy tears, and craving peach cobbler every night for a month straight.

With this one, all I wanted were frosted pickles. And I wasn't kidding, as much as I wished otherwise.

Marcy caught me glancing toward the fridge and smirked. "Go on. You know you want one."

"I don't know what you're talking about," I said primly.

"Liar. I've seen the jar. You hide it behind the butter like it's state secrets."

Before I could protest, the back door opened, and just like always, my heart jumped when I saw Wesley.

He walked in like he owned the place. Technically, he half did since he was my husband, and I became Marcy's partner in the bakery two years ago.

His gaze landed on me first, like always. And despite the bump, the flour, and the pink icing in my hair, the heat in his eyes hadn't changed one bit since the first time he walked into the bakery.

"Security check?" Marcy called, not even glancing up from the dough she was working on.

"Something like that," he muttered.

I grinned and waddled—yes, waddled—around the counter to meet him. His arm wrapped around my waist the second I got close, tugging me against his chest as though he hadn't just seen me a few hours ago when he'd dropped Sarah and me off at the bakery.

"Hey, sunshine."

"Hey, yourself." I leaned up and kissed his scruffy jaw. "We're a little messy today."

His amber eyes cut to the counter, where our daughter was now taste-testing frosting with a spatula like it was her job.

"You don't say." His voice was dry, but the corner of his mouth twitched.

"She's got your sweet tooth."

"She's got your everything else," he retorted.

I didn't argue since Sarah was very much a mini me, much to Wesley's satisfaction.

His hand slid over the bump between us, gentle and reverent, and I swore the baby kicked for him on purpose.

"She tried to eat frosting on a pickle this morning," I complained. "It's like the baby's already a bad influence."

"Or a genius. You never know. Frosted pickles could be the next big thing."

Marcy groaned. "Please don't say that. We'll end up with a viral request, and I'll have to quit the bakery in protest."

Wesley just chuckled, the sound deep and warm. Then he bent down and pressed a kiss to my belly. "How's my littlest girl?"

"Wiggly. And apparently opinionated."

He straightened, pulling me flush against him. "Just like her mama."

I rolled my eyes. "Flatter me again, and I'll let you take over the piping bag."

"I'd rather take you home," he said, voice dipping low enough to make my toes curl.

"Tempting," I breathed. "But your daughter is waiting for her cupcake."

"Fine. We'll spoil her first." He leaned in closer. "Then I get you."

My toes curled at the sensual promise in his deep voice.

Across the counter, our daughter beamed and held up a very pink cupcake. "Daddy! Dis one for you!"

Wesley took a bite out of it and flashed her a gentle smile. "Best cupcake I've ever had."

I was incredibly thankful I saw that random social media post about Country Crust's soft opening way back when. Then again, I had a feeling I would've met Wesley some other way if I hadn't since we were meant to be together.

Always.

Phoenix is about to meet his match in the woman who showed up before the wedding and needed to talk to the Iron Rogues treasurer!

And if you join our newsletter, you'll get a FREE copy of The Virgin's Guardian, which was banned on Amazon.

ABOUT THE AUTHOR

The writing duo of Elle Christensen and Rochelle Paige team up under the Fiona Davenport pen name to bring you sexy, insta-love stories filled with alpha males. If you want a quick & dirty read with a guaranteed happily ever after, then give Fiona Davenport a try!

Printed in Great Britain
by Amazon

61950359R00097